Ranendra is a Hindi writer and critic. He was the editor of *Panchayati Raj: Hashiye Se Hukumat Tak* and the *Jharkhand Encyclopedia*. His previously published work includes the bestseller, *Gayab Hota Desh*, a collection of stories, *Raat Baaki Evam Anya Kahaniya*, and a book of poetry, *Thoda Sa Eshtri Hona Chahta Hoon*. He lives in Ranchi.

Rajesh Kumar has written short stories and poems in both Hindi and English. Some of his important translations from Hindi into English include Sanjeev's *Jungle Jahan Shuroo Hota Hai* and Mahua Maji's *Main, Borishailla*. He is the editor of *TLV*, a refereed research journal for English Literature & Language. Currently, he is head, Department of English, Vinobha Bhave University, Hazaribag, and director, University Law College.

Lords of the Global Village

RANENDRA

Translated by

RAJESH KUMAR

SPEAKING
TIGER

SPEAKING TIGER PUBLISHING PVT. LTD
4381/4 Ansari Road, Daryaganj,
New Delhi–110002, India

First published in Hindi as *Global Gaon ke Devta* by
Bharatiya Jnanpith 2010

Published in English by Speaking Tiger 2017

ISBN: 978-81-93314-15-9
eISBN: 978-93-86338-43-3

10 9 8 7 6 5 4 3 2 1

Typeset in Adobe Garamond Pro by SÜRYA, New Delhi
Printed at Thomson Press India Ltd.

Translator's Note

Lords of the Global Village is a tale of our times, written by Ranendra, a sensitive and creative soul, who has lived and felt the realities of life in a largely tribal area. The original Hindi work, *Global Gaaon ke Devta,* is a moving account of the inequities that the people of this area suffer as a part of their assimilation through an unequal social, economic and cultural process, in the name of privatization and globalization. Naturally, when Ranendraji approached me to translate the book, I felt it was an opportunity to reiterate anthropological facts, the ground realities of extremism and administrative responses.

The author has used very simple language, swinging organically between tenses, structures and dialects. It was a tough task to let its uniqueness seep through into the English language (which now belongs to us Indians too). I have experimented with the upright and colloquial forms in the narrative, using many nouns from the tribal dialects, as well as from Hindi, as Ranendraji did in the original, to carry an authentic touch. In addition, the idiomatic earthiness of Hindi and English are somewhat different, and sometimes what is being said in one language cannot be fully conveyed in the other. A glossary has been placed at the end of the work for readers unfamiliar with the languages.

I won't claim that this is the best of translations, because judgment is a subjective matter and one's writing can always be improved upon by a better writer. This is the case with every book, in every language, and this very temptation for improvement and excellence constitutes the core of human existence and survival. Like the Asurs in Ranendraji's novel—Lalchan, Balchan and Doctor Ram Kumar—language faces onslaughts and changes continuously, but will persist as long as humans feel the urge to communicate.

—RAJESH KUMAR

I girdle the wind, the water,
The earth I secure and the sky,
Nine forests, ten flanks,
One lakh kine,
And a lakh and a quarter the herbs.
I hold down nine lakh witches,
Ten lakh ghosts,
The Thakur Deva of the three realms,
Darha and Masan I bind.
Who commands?
The Lord All-compassionate—Mahadeva does it,
Who straps them?
Paat God—Sarna Mother does.
Who secures?
I, their Bhagat, do it.
Even when the dry dung cakes are blown away,
The livestock and the trees too,
The rocks as well as the mountains;
My words shall not fail.

—An Asur mantra

1

Should this appointment letter send me into the throes of ecstasy? Or should it depress me? What should I do? A ray of light has appeared after a long, dark night of unemployment—a night of privations, insult and humiliation. I have finally landed a job. I ought to go crazy with joy, dance, leap! But the location of the school I am to join has driven me into an abyss of despair. The Barwe district is, by the shortest route, no less than 300 kilometres from our hometown. And to make matters worse, this school is in some damned miserable place called Bhaunrapaat in the Koelbigha block. It stands in the middle of a forest, up in the hills. PTG Girls' Residential School. I will be a science teacher for girls from tribal families. Curse my luck! I feel like thumping my head in despair. Why does this always happen to me? Is it because Ma has been saving the last roti for me everyday, and the proverbial bad luck is coming true?

Ramadhar Babu, the MLA, was related by marriage to a village uncle; they were each other's samdhis. The very next morning, we visited his house with the traditional complimentary box of seer and a quarter kilo of laddus.

'The boy's job has come with your blessing, now his posting is also within your powers. No one but you can rescue him!' Babuji whined before the MLA.

'Look here, Samdhi', my uncle took charge. 'We have come with full faith in you. The boy has to be married off. How is he supposed to live with his family in that goddamn forest? How will the daughter-in-law stay there? His deliverance is in your hands'.

'Let's see what I can do. Guptaji! Where are you, PA Sahib? Hoye?'

'Sir! I am right by your side.'

'Hey! Samdhiji is here personally. And look at this boy. Such a fine lad! Why should he go to this jungle? He must be posted in the capital or at least in his district. Who should we call? Education Secretary?'

'No, sir. Director Mishraji from the Welfare Department will do.'

'Call him up. Hold on, it is not easy to contact him at this hour. But yes, we can do this. I have to go to the Secretariat today. Remind me after my meeting with the Transport Secretary. Let's get it finalized with the director.' The MLA flung his stolid assurance towards us. 'You can return happily, Samdhi. Go take a cool bath and enjoy a hearty meal. It will be done this very day!'

We came back in high spirits, but nothing had

materialized even by the date set for me to join. Finally, dejected and morose, at the end of June, I moved from a bus to a Trekker and then onto a bauxite-laden truck, lurching through the winding mountain road, until I came to Bhaunrapaat. The school's teaching staff consisted of two female teachers and the headmistress. The clerk, Sahu Babu, was male. This brightened my mood up a little. The headmistress and the teachers would commute from the town. Sahu Babu's residence was in Sakhuapaat Bazaar, closer by. The dilapidated teachers' quarters on the campus had never been lived in.

Cobwebs and dust lay in every nook and cranny and a crumbling, rotten door and window panels. A female peon stayed in the corner house. With the sweeper's help, she somehow managed to clean my accommodation and make it habitable in one day. I was still counting on the MLA. The school closed at three o'clock. The teachers had to catch the last bus from Sakhuapaat. I rode pillion on Sahuji's bicycle to the small settlement, around 5 kilometres away. Although the truck had passed this way in the morning, I had hardly glanced at anything.

There was a bustling market. Close to it were the offices and the quarters of the Shindalco mines. A number of officers and junior staff lived here. There were a number of smaller bauxite-mine bureaus. There was a Gramin bank, government health centres, government buildings, tiny hotels, grocery stores, kiosks selling tea and paan—

altogether, it was a lively spot. Sakhuapaat was a regular stopping point for the empty trucks coming from below and the bauxite-ferrying trucks that travelled from the mines. Getting challans issued from the Shindalco office was a time-consuming affair. However, the market remained full of life.

Sahuji was trying to enlighten me with sundry facts about the place but I caught only snatches. I was not even certain I was listening. All my senses were focused on the STD booth. Calling my home and calling Guptaji, the MLA's PA, every morning and evening, were an obsession for me.

Back in Bhaunrapaat, the plateau at the top of the sprawling, winding hills looked desolate. There were clumps of forest now and then and fallow, barren fields stretching in all directions, dotted with open-cast bauxite mines. Craters were left where all the bauxite ore had been excavated; they yawned everywhere—Mother Earth's face was pitted with smallpox. Not a single civilized soul was in view. Silence reigned supreme at the onset of dusk.

The power situation was erratic. The peon, Etwari, generously baked rotis for me. Her husband was a miner, a quarry worker. He would flop down in bed, arriving drunk after the day's bone-breaking labour. I have never come across such a quiet fellow. Although we used to walk together to a mountain spring in the jungle every morning for ablutions and our daily baths, he would remain engrossed in chewing on a twig brush or fill his mouth with khaini. Apparently he did not like conversation. I, too, had never been a garrulous sort. At home, my mother and sisters called me 'Ghunna' (introvert) instead of Munna. After a while, I noticed he looked sullen sometimes, because Etwari often offered me more help than was needed. I was in an unfamiliar place, surrounded by total strangers, and so I grew worried and cut down my contact with Etwari, responding to her only in monosyllables.

The girls' hostel was on the campus. They had a separate mess with two female cooks from Bhaunrapaat village. However, I felt it was improper to go to the hostel at night for dinner, so I had to make do with the rotis cooked by Etwari.

One night, I was staying with Sahuji at Sakhuapaat. The quarters belonged to the halka karmachari of the Koelbigha block, but he did not live here and had rented them out. Late in the night, a commotion in the other room broke my sleep; there was pandemonium and noisy fighting. Finally, I figured out that a contractor—Ansari Sahib—and his consort, Ramrati, were the reason. Their friends were invited every evening. Wine flowed freely. After everyone was drunk, the party broke up with such brawling. The routine continued uninterrupted three hundred and sixty-five days a year. There were also arrangements for upgraded entertainment. A live blue film was shown after the commotion, with no ticket necessary! It was played under the full glare of the electric bulb, with the doors and windows flung open. 'They are absolutely shameless, these two,' was Sahuji's commentary.

I somehow managed to survive the first week in Bhaunrapaat, amid the forests and the mines in the hills, completely cut off from civilization, finding it impossible to let go of the image of the MLA's house in the capital. Let alone the girls in the classes, I was not even properly acquainted with the headmistress and my colleagues. If I closed my eyes, I could hardly recall their features. The only intimacy I had was with Sahuji and Etwari. I was thoroughly disgusted.

The evenings were the most onerous. After darkness fell, it was hard to find a truck in Sakhuapaat to travel down to Bhaunrapaat. I was forced to spend my evenings on campus. The shrill chirp of the crickets was often drowned in the bawling of Etwari's children or the bickering of the girls in the hostel. But as night approached, the song of the crickets and the baying of the jackals smothered all other sounds. My heart felt leaden, as if it were weighed down by a wet, sodden blanket. Misery pressed down on me. My eyes would fill with tears when I remembered home and I yearned to just break away and bolt off from there.

One morning, I had just returned after my dip in the mountain spring and was changing my clothes when someone rushed into my room unannounced, stumbling, banging against the door and the bucket, and clutching me tightly in a desperate hold.

2

His unexpected entrance unsettled me, but the poor fellow himself was shaking in terror. It took me a couple of seconds to compose myself. I led him to the chowki to sit down and gave him some water to sip. Then I looked closely at him. He was quite fair, around thirty years old. He wore a white dhoti, badly torn, and a cream polyester kurta, also ripped to shreds. He had bleeding wounds on his head and face, the blood seeping from his head on to his face and dripping down.

A stranger in my room and in such a bizarre condition! What should I say to him? I was wondering what to do when Etwari came in.

'Hey! Dada, Lalchan Dada!' Etwari was distraught at seeing his wretched state. 'Where did it happen? How? Who did it?' Her questions were not out of place. But he did not utter a syllable. She wetted a towel and gave it to Dada. Lalchan's trembling stopped and he looked less tense. But there was no use wiping his face. The blood seeping from his head would only start flowing again.

Etwari burnt an old piece of cloth and held the warm ash against his head wound. Then the bleeding finally stopped. I took out a piece of alum from my shaving kit and, dipping it in water, rubbed it on the scratches and cuts on his face and limbs. It proved effective. Etwari brought two soothing cups of steaming black tea.

Etwari said, 'He's the Pradhan of our village, Ambatoli. Lalchan Asur, Baiga Baba's eldest son.' I had already heard that the region was inhabited by Asurs, but had always thought they would be dark-skinned giants with protruding teeth and horns growing out of their heads. But she had called this handsome man Lalchan Asur. Lalchan's looks dispelled that myth. The stories I had heard about them in my childhood seemed like tall tales now.

Etwari's husband, Gandoor, peered into the room. He had his bicycle and lunch-box and seemed ready to leave for duty. He greeted Lalchan with a johar. God knows what they talked of in their unfamiliar tongue, but Gandoor propped the bicycle against the wall and after giving Etwari some instructions, walked off. I followed nothing except the johar. Etwari told me that they were speaking in the Asuri tongue. They, too, were Asurs.

Lalchan Dada was to be carried on the bicycle to Sakhuapaat, to Ram Kumar Doctor's. The pain would subside after the pills and injections he would get there.

Everything seemed startlingly new to me, as if I had woken up after a week's slumber. This svelte, comely woman, Etwari, was also an Asur! The revelation amazed me. I had been watching her for a week; she had no long, pointed claws or blood-sucking fangs. What misconceptions I used to have! I was sorely ashamed of myself.

I put Lalchan on the rear seat of the bicycle and pedalled towards Sakhuapaat. We did not talk much on the way. When asked about how he had received the injuries, he simply told me that I would not understand. Such incidents often took place during the paddy planting, he added.

The connection between the planting and the injuries vexed me further. After giving him medication, an injection and dressing the wounds, Doctor Ram Kumar explained the mystery. He was jovial and good-looking, the same age as Lalchan; equally fair, but taller. He was a registered practitioner, from the Kanari Babuani Tola, an area lower down the hill. The two of them were hardly four or five years older than me, so we became very close in no time at all.

'A superstition runs in the region, although it has gotten weaker with time. Still, stray incidents take place during the kharif season. Man's life appears to have no value at all here,' Ram Kumar tried to explain. 'Actually, some people still believe that one can harvest a bumper crop if the rice seedlings are soaked in human blood. Many murikatwas wander around during this season, looking for heads to hunt. With a razor-sharp steel hatchet in one hand and a sack in the other, the murikatwas stalk their prey in deserted spots, far from their own villages. Lalchan had an encounter with a murikatwa this morning. The poor man sped off on his bicycle when he saw an unfamiliar person holding a sack and lurking. The killer caught hold of the end of his dhoti. The dhoti ripped off and he ran away, tripping, abandoning the bicycle. He hurt himself when he slipped down the hill.'

My head reeled. What kind of world was this?

'It is damn difficult to survive on this paat, Master Sahib, but death comes so very easily.' Ram Kumar anticipated my thoughts. 'You have just arrived here. You'll see how hard life is when one has to sustain oneself on a single, rain-fed maize crop. If the support offered by the jobs in the mines and the jungle had not been there, the people would have migrated to Assam or Bhutan. But the mines have brought ruin as well as livelihood. For the last twenty-five to thirty years, the cavernous ditches that the mine owners have left behind fill up with water every monsoon and turn into breeding grounds for mosquitoes. Cerebral malaria is endemic here. You may bump into a murikatwa only once in a year or two, but the other killer is a familiar, regular visitor.'

'What about Singhji? Murikatwas can be seen on every village market day.' Lalchan's complexion had returned to normal.

'Oh yes! I can show you the lone murikatwa of our area tomorrow in the haat, Budhram Singh Kherwar from Kamti village. He has bulging, red eyes, always rolled up as if he were drunk. His looks are so dreadful that even a stranger can put two and two together. But he has justification for why he is that way. There is a cave around 70 to 80 feet up the hillock by his village. The path to it is pretty steep. A new fellow would never make it. Singhji says that it is the Devi-thaan. When the Devi calls for a sacrifice, the sound of drum-beats rises from the cave. Then we know the time has come. In desperation, we have to venture far from our thana area to get hold of the puja, the sacrificial victim. After the sacrifice of the devotee, the drum-beats cease, all by themselves. Tell me, how can an entire village invite the displeasure of the Devi? We are helpless. Since you are an educated fellow, you might say it's all rubbish. But this is no joke! You will only realize it when you start suffering. Now you get how and why no one dares to ask about Singhji!'

The doctor continued, 'Lalchan told me that there is a village called Katiya in the Kamti panchayat. The practice was popular there till recently. But now there are road-*shod*. Schools and anganbaris have started functioning. People have become literate. When they began visiting more advanced places, things became better. But if you ask them about it, they will get annoyed. They will convince you that the object of sacrifice comes to the village in the puja season himself. It is all thanks to the grace of the Goddess. No sooner does some lunatic, raving fellow arrive in the village on that occasion, that we understand that he is the sacrificial object come at the command of the Devi. But now we only make a tiny cut on his little finger and offer a few drops of blood at the Devi-thaan. The Devi is pleased with the sparse offering and the bhagat comes back to his senses. You can't fathom it. The matter is related to rituals, devotion and devotees and all that. You'll never understand it.

'Whosoever the people of Katiya are, they have never harmed the people of this area, not even with their little finger. But what about these hundreds of yawning holes dotting the paat? So many petitions have been submitted. I wrote many of the applications myself. When the very first clause in the agreement states that the ditches have to be filled after excavation, why has it not been done for scores of years? I feel the government is dithering and has an ulterior motive. It intends to decimate the population on the paat. The sooner they are gone, the easier it will be to extract the bauxite.' Ram Kumar's anger spilled over.

'But if this were the intention of the government, why would it start a residential school here?' I asked, intrigued.

'Hey, Master Sahib! You talk of the residential school for the tribal folks! First go visit the world-famous school at Patharpaat. Then you will find out what a real school is and what a sham one is!' Lalchan threw down the gauntlet.

'Tomorrow is Sunday. Rumjhum will take you to Patharpaat. He will be at your place early in the morning. He is your age and has an Honours degree in Sanskrit. His father is a school teacher, but he has not got a job yet. God knows what has struck him, but you will find him going to Patharpaat to gaze at the school all the time. He's quite learned. You'll enjoy his company.'

Doctor Sahib had made fine arrangements for my Sunday. I had taken the entrance examination for Patharpaat Vidyalaya years ago, but had failed to qualify. Now that I was so close, I wanted to see it. I came back to my room to wait for Rumjhum Asur's arrival.

3

Generally, Sundays for me are days of indolence, slumber and time spent in bed. I relish getting up late and savouring the lassitude of sleep. Then I take a bath in slow motion. A sumptuous breakfast is followed by taking up a favourite book, lolling in bed and tossing from side to side. I read ten pages and then take a ten-minute siesta. It's a duet of study and sleep. To hell with the dreary, onerous, loneliness-laced Sunday!

But the torpor of sleep was gone today. Bubbling with energy, I took a bath early in the morning. Etwari made rice instead of the usual fare. I was done with my meal by nine-thirty. I was dressed up and feeling restless. My eyes kept wandering to the gate of the campus. I walked out of the room and began to pace up and down.

Etwari sensed my eagerness. She told me that Rumjhum's house was pretty far away. The paat is not all level. There are small valleys between the ranges, half-a-mile wide and one or two miles long. The rice fields of the Asurs are situated in the depressions between two hills.

The road to Rumjhum's village, Kandapaat, lies across two such vales and hills. Since it was Sunday, he might have woken up late. He might arrive any moment now, after enjoying a leisurely meal.

Rumjhum did come late. Finally, I had gone back to my room to flick through the pages of a book. My yearning to find out about the Asurs had now grown stronger. The school had a rich library. The woman who had been headmistress before Madam Minj had loved books. She had amassed a fine collection of volumes during her seven-year tenure. I had issued all the books on the Asurs and now, from Verrier Elwin to A.C. Roy, all of them were piled on the table in my room.

Rumjhum arrived at around half-past ten. He had a dark, shining face, sharp nose and expressive eyes, a curly beard and a mane of curly hair flowing to his shoulders. He did not appear older than me. During our conversation, he told me that he had completed his graduation two years before me.

We walked down to the road to ask for a lift from a bauxite truck moving towards Patharpaat More. Rumjhum told me our destination was barely 10 to 12 kilometres away, but overloaded bauxite trucks had ravaged the road. The government wanted the mining companies to share the cost of the road repairs. The companies felt that the roads were the government's responsibility. We paid taxes (they thought), why should we take pains for repairs? And so the potholes and ditches in the roads were merely filled with laterite in the rainy season, and the workers thought their job was complete. It took a full, jolting hour to travel 10 kilometres. The officers from the company were not bothered at all. They simply drove all over the fields and the fallows in their Jonga-*Mongas*, off-road hunting jeeps. 'Their time is valuable, brother. They are not workless, worthless, witless bums like us,' Rumjhum said.

We reached Patharpaat, chatting about diverse topics. The truck had to make the descent from there and travel about 60 kilometres to the railway junction where the bauxite would be loaded on freight cars to be transported to aluminium factories. We had to get down at the fork.

Patharpaat was quite popular with Bengali tourists. Quite a number of small and big vehicles were passing to and fro, but Rumjhum did not think it proper to ask for a lift for the sake of a kilometre or two. We moved off the road, taking a shortcut on foot. Our talk resumed. Rumjhum liked to go into every subject in depth.

'The place where our bauxite is carted away to be processed into aluminium, around 200 kilometres from here, is called the Silver City of India. I got a chance to go there once. I saw a beautiful, lush green colony full of flowers and parks. Wonderful schools, glittering malls, club house, yoga centre, library, sports fields and endless other facilities. Gorgeous women walking with cute dogs, and kids fair and cuddly like snowballs, and colourful cars. It was as if Indra's royal court had alighted on earth. Now that you have come to live on the paat, Master Sahib, you will learn everything slowly. Our women waste half their lives fetching water and wood. Don't ask about the troubles during the rains. The hundreds of ditches formed by the abandoned mines become large lakes. It becomes difficult to differentiate between our children and pigs wallowing in the mud. In sharp contrast, you will find an array of sumptuous dishes in the company's guest-house. No, I am not speaking metaphorically. It's absolutely true. It was hard to choose a dish. My tummy got upset in a single day. In our houses, we get blisters on our tongues trying to eat real corn. In most of our huts, even a dish of rice and pulses is nothing short of a festival delicacy.'

His anger was certainly not misplaced. Rumjhum's voice quavered and his eyes grew moist. We slowed down and sat on a rock. The atmosphere became heavy. We avoided looking at each other.

I spoke after a while, trying to lighten the mood by changing the topic. 'The second name of your people is really astonishing, Rumjhum Bhai.'

Rumjhum burst into a laugh. 'You're right. The word "Asur" reminds you of two things. One is the stories of giants, demons and fiends heard during one's childhood. What terrible descriptions! Ten to 12 feet tall. Protruding teeth. An assortment of weapons in their hands. Cannibals, devotees of Lord Shiva, brawny, yet able to be slaughtered.

The curtain scene of all the god–demon struggles is predestined! The other is the photographs of loincloth-wearing Asur men and bare-breasted women in the 1926, 1946 and 1966 anthropology books. Now you decide, Master Sahib, what we are.'

His face darkened, his voice flattened. But he braced himself and started speaking again.

'The struggle between the gods and demons had befuddled me too, Master Sahib. That's why I chose Sanskrit for my subject. The books collected by Baba must have played a vital role in the selection. Although Baba is a science teacher, he has gathered a number of books on religion and history in search of his roots.'

We got up. The sun was filtering through the leaves. We walked faster to escape the growing heat.

'We Asurs have three branches,' Rumjhum resumed. 'Bir Asur, Agaria Asur and Birijia Asur. The word "Bir" does not imply "brave" but is related somehow to the forest. In the ancient Assyrian–Babylonian civilization, "Asur" meant "a strong man". In our civilization too, Sayanacharya has called the Asurs mighty, enlightened foe-slayers and protectors. Around 150 shlokas in the Rigveda treat the Asurs as gods. Mitra, Varun, Agni, Rudra—all of them are called Asur. Later on, the meaning shifted and the Asurs began to be equated with demons.

'The similarity between the names Angira Rishi and Agaria is remarkable,' he continued. 'Angira Rishi claims to be born from fire. The Agaria Asurs also make the same claim. It was Angira who first discovered fire. The story of the discovery of fire and the fight with the gods is prevalent in many countries. In the Greek legend, Prometheus steals fire from heaven and the gods punish him. In the local legend, this punishment is dispensed by Sing-Bonga—the Sun God. The struggle between the Surs (gods) and the Asurs (demons) is a complex riddle. Some day, we can sit together to solve it. Was it a fight involving the Palaeolithic ore-smelting people? The stem "Su" means "production", and is included in "Sur". Therefore, was it a fight between the forest-razing, cultivator-producers on the one hand, and the iron smelters dependent on the charcoal made from sakhua trees on the other? Jhum cultivation is done by cutting and burning down forests. A forest fire spreads quickly. "Vishnu" has multiple meanings, including "expanding" and "yajna". Naturally, people dependent on jungles for food and livelihood would take offence at the gutting of forests—you may call the process "yajna" or "Vishnu"; what difference would it make? This might be the reason behind the fights. There can be any number of explanations…

'But we'll talk about it later. Let's visit the school first.'

The gate of Patharpaat School was up ahead. The campus was so big that two or three villages the size of Bhaunrapaat could easily have fit into it. It was picturesque—full of greenery, a planned campus. As soon as we entered, my eyes fell on the statue of a tribal woman walking to the market. A child was tied to her back, she held a hen in one hand and a small bundle of firewood on her head. She looked almost alive, charming.

The brightest boys of the state came to study in these huge buildings. They were taught by the worthiest, best-paid teachers. They had to become administrators some day. The hostel system was unique. Each hostel had a teacher's family attached to it. The family played the role of parents for the boarders of that particular hostel and the children grew up in their care. Sports, painting, music, debate—every aspect of personality development was taken care of here. Doctor Sahib was absolutely right—this was a real school!

But Rumjhum's concerns were different. 'More than a hundred Asur families were uprooted to build this school. They still inhabit the adjacent areas. They haven't gone very far; the whole population of the Asurs, Birijias and the Korbas is settled within a radius of 20 to 22 kilometres. Go through the admission registers of the last thirty years, and you will find that not a single child from a single tribal family has studied in this school. I have tried my best. For the last two or three years I have been trying to get an appointment as a casual teacher here, but there is no hope. Why do they hate even our shadows? Brought up on rice and starch, in the care of semi-literate and illiterate teachers, our children will be nothing more than skilled labourers, peons or clerks from the sham schools. This is our status. They erect a Taj Mahal-like school on our bosom to show us where we stand.'

The atmosphere became heavy again.

4

With every passing day, I grew fonder of my Bhaunrapaat School. I developed a liking for the headmistress, the teachers and the little girls, the classes and the obvious trickery of Sahuji, the clerk. Etwari already had my favour, and I began to admire her husband, Gandoor, too. We became pals quickly. Every morning, while walking to and fro from the jungle spring, we would talk about everything under the sun. The story of how he got his name was really bizarre. The children born to his parents before Gandoor had not survived. They had died within a month or two of their births. So once Gandoor was born, his parents resorted to black magic. The moment he was born, Gandoor's Aaji, his grandmother, wrapped him in a piece of cloth and put him on the garbage heap, or gandoor, outside the house, bringing him back after a little while. This is how he became Gandoor.

But there was a rub in my new-found cheerfulness, and it was the irritating memory of Patharpaat Vidyalaya. I could see the contrast between a real school and a sham one. This was when Rumjhum's bitter, candid statement came to mind. And then I would suddenly find Bhaunrapaat School no better than a pigsty. Half-constructed buildings, a poorly built hostel and teachers' quarters like hen coops. The part which should have been immaculate was in fact the filthiest. It was hard to decide whether the mess in the girls' hostel was ever cleaned or not. Nobody was willing to own up to its responsibility, but everyone was after the chance to look after the mess purchases—there lay the real profit.

The headmistress would get annoyed with me. 'It is enough that these eaters of boiled corn get rice and pulses here. Why do you look at it from your perspective? Do they ever get kheer and puri in their homes? Then why are you dying to reform the mess system?' But my hue and cry had an effect and a little cleanliness became visible. The children started getting not just the turmeric water that was passed off as pulses, but also some real grains in it. They also started receiving two slices of potato among the vegetables and green spinach.

Lalchan and Rumjhum brought out another skeleton. Bhaunrapaat School had actually been founded for the girls from tribal families, but the number of the girls from Asur and Birijia families did not add up to even 10 per cent. A majority of the students belonged to the villages and castes of the headmistress and the teachers—Oraon–Kharia and Kherwar.

I examined the registers carefully. The allegation was true. Once again, I had a row with the headmistress, Madam Minj. When Lalchan and Rumjhum joined forces with me, she gave in, 'Go ahead! Go try. If their girls come, why won't we admit them? We certainly would. But the half-yearly exam is at hand. Everybody will have to take the test. Classes will be allotted on the basis of performance in the test. I won't admit them to a class simply because you say I should or because they are growing up.'

We took up the challenge. It became our sacred duty to visit the tolas every morning and evening. Soma and Bhikha, two intermediate-pass boys from Lalchan's village, accompanied us. Finally, our month-long labour bore fruit. Sixty-seven girls from the Asur, Birijia and Korba tribal families were admitted to the school.

But making the arrangements for teaching them was complicated. Madam Minj and the rest of the teachers had their families to look after. There appeared to be no solution to the problem of their coming late and leaving early. The only way out was for Sahu, Etwari and Rumjhum Babu to also take classes. They had to do a self-appraisal to decide which classes they would be taking up. However, it worked, and I enjoyed a little bit of satisfaction at seeing it. Gradually, the set-up became acceptable.

I spruced up my room after collecting my first salary. A tube light, a portable TV and a gas cylinder were brought in. In the evenings, Etwari's children would do their homework in my room, sitting on a mat. Gandoor would also come by after dinner to watch TV, and Etwari would follow with her needlework. Now the house looked like a home.

In my dreams too, Bhaunrapaat began to eclipse my home town. The memories of my friends from college and university receded. The girls from the past also faded from my dreams. In their place, there would be Madam Minj, now smiling, now testy. My nightly visions were also merrily inhabited by the heavy bosom of the Hindi teacher, Mary Kachchap, the sashaying of the large-hipped English teacher, Sushma Singh Kherwar, and the lilaceous Etwari.

5

A valuable result of my campaign for the admission of Asur girls was that I was now accepted in many of their families. Between us, there grew an intimacy that is hard to imagine even among many close relatives. My rigorously doled out smiles brought me into the doors, courtyards and kitchens of certain houses.

Rumjhum's ayo (mother) and Lalchan Dada's gomkain (wife) became my cherished acquaintances, closer to me than my own kin. The two had one thing in common: they were living symbols of tireless labour. They never looked weary. I often stayed back to chat with them at night. The male family members would enjoy their meals, get into bed, gossip and start snoring. But the women would continue cleaning the utensils, ovens and the kitchen.

In the wee hours of the night, when the morning star was still twinkling in the night sky, and the sunrise was far off, the song of the wooden dhenki would begin to rise. It was the hour to pound paddy for the daytime meal. Then the women would carry the bigger pots to a stream or spring a mile downhill in order to clean them, and return with the rising sun, the vessels filled with water and shining from brisk scrubbing. They seemed to be in a race with the Sun God, Sing-Bonga, as if saying let's see who touches the threshold first! After this, they'd be occupied with arranging firewood. This would be followed by feeding the cattle and cooking. They would send the children to school and the men to their jobs. Only then would they take a bath and wash their clothes. Finally, they would eat their first morsel, no earlier than noon. Even after all this, there was no respite. Much, in fact most, of the work in the fields was also done by them. The men would plough the fields, dig and harrow. If they felt like it, they would plant the seedlings or help with the harvesting. But the dozens of small and big tasks related to cultivation were the responsibility of the women. Laughing and singing, they did the work cheerfully.

When Lalchan Da's gomkain, Rumjhum's ayo, and all other Asur women, perspiring profusely, laughed and chuckled, Mother Earth and Sarna Mai would join them. After all, Sarna Mai and Mother Earth were also women!

Large mud houses were dotted across the paat, each within a big enclosure. Rooms—the courtyard and the cow pen in one corner, hen coops on the veranda. These cows and calves, he-goats and she-goats, hens and pigs were not merely animals, but also passbooks for the tribal folks. Distress or illness, weddings or nuptials were borne and solemnized on their strength. If it were required, the creatures were sold in the haat.

The women coated the outer walls of the enclosure with soil. In this community, women were called siyani—worldly-wise—not janani. The word 'janani' was parochial, binding them to the role of begetters of progeny; on the other hand, 'siyani' symbolized their vast experience and wisdom. The siyani women-folk knew in which taand, which don, to find the black, yellow and white soils for coating the house. The upper portions of the terrace fields, humidity-starved, were called 'taand', while the lower, water-rich part was called 'don'.

The walls were first coated diligently with black soil. The floor would also be coated and then polished so painstakingly with a smooth stone that it would shine like glossy cement. A layer of white soil was then put on the black soil of the walls. Then the palms would be rotated across them to create circular patterns, bearing the imprint of the artists' hands. This unique hand motif was visible not only on the walls and above the doors, but also in the fields and barns, the woods and the orchards, the mines, rivers and streams, the chuan or springs, the pajhara or waterfalls—everywhere. Sometimes it appeared as if this earth, the sun, moon, stars, the whole cosmos, our own Milky Way and the infinite Milky Ways in the infinite cosmoses in creation had all been dancing like the pirouette of a woman's hand since time immemorial. The celestial dance bears the imprint of a woman's palm.

Lalchan Dada's family was bigger than Rumjhum's. It consisted of Lalachan's ayo and baba, the younger brothers, Balchan and Ramchan, their wives and the two or three children belonging to each couple. Lalchan's daughters, Kavita and Namita, were day scholars at my school, and they walked from home every day. The son, Ramesh, was in Sakhuapaat High School. Lalchan's baba was Ambatoli's baiga—the witch man of the village. Baba was an influential fellow. The Asurs venerated him. He owned large tracts of land—fifteen to twenty acres of taand fields on the paat and many acres of fertile rice fields in the basin between the two hills. They did not lack food at home.

In every village, there were a few families who managed to harvest crops round the year. But most of the residents did not have the kind of land that would allow them to reap maize the whole year round. The families whose men went to work in the mines somehow managed two square meals a day, but in less fortunate homes, the members had to scour the jungle to make ends meet. Mahua, jackfruit, different types of sprigs and herbs—everything was used as food. One of the more bitter roots was really hard to make edible. At first it was boiled with the ashes from firewood. Then it was put under the spout of a small stream, from which two or three thin tongues of water would splash down. The bitterness would not be completely washed away, but at least it would become palatable.

Balchan, Lalchan Da's younger brother, was quite hefty and tall. After failing the matriculation exam once, he never went back to school. Instead, he immersed himself in household work and agriculture. He would labour to the hilt and eat to his heart's content. In fact, it was thanks to Balchan that Lalchan Da roamed about the village without the least worry.

The other brother, Ramchan, a wispy, emaciated fellow, was quite the opposite. He was very good at studies. When he was an undergraduate, he fell prey to all kinds of addictions like khaini, tobacco and gutka. Once, when he came home during a vacation, Lalchan took him to task and the boy retaliated by missing his examination on purpose. He then took to loafing about.

Lalchan's house was by the road. There was a large piece of land between the road and the house, which served as the barnyard. Lalchan had had the foresight to get the government community hall built at the end of the barnyard that lay near the road. The advantage was that whenever a government employee like the karamachari, panchayat sewak or jan sewak came to the paat, he stayed in the community hall and Lalchan Da could easily elicit information on any new government projects. The customary snacks served at Lalchan Da's house entailed that such projects would go to the poor families of the village, when they were guided there by an influential man like him.

Now, my Saturday evenings and Sundays were spent either at Ambatoli or in Rumjhum's village, Kandapaat.

Due to Gandoor's company on the school campus, I would join them sometimes, on Saturdays or Sundays, to drink hanriya. Etwari used herbs ground with powdered rice to ferment boiled rice. I had occasionally drunk bhang in my own home and village. The intoxication produced by hanriya was lighter. It made you a little tipsy after one or two dona-fuls; the donas were made from sakhua leaves. Sometimes, Etwari also joined us. The hanriya-induced light-headedness had two benefits. The first was that they would forget I was a teacher and they the lowly peon and labourers; secondly, they would treat me as their equal. The feeling of my being an outsider began to diminish, gradually.

One particular Saturday night, we had a sitting at Ambatoli. We drank hanriya and then enjoyed a feast of jackfruit and boiled rice. Lalchan's wife, Bhauji, was very fond of me. Whenever I visited her house after a gap of five or ten days, she would observe mirthfully that I had grown thinner. Since Etwari was related to her sister-in-law, Bhauji would tease me, saying that Etwari had not been feeding me well and had been gobbling away my portions instead; that was why she was growing fatter by the day. She would keep pulling my leg in this fashion. If she were in a light mood, she would hum dewar–bhabhi songs while serving me, often breaking out in a ditty:

Why brother-in-law, do you look so sad,
Why is your heart so dry?
You look sad because you are hungry,
You look sad because you are thirsty.

It was thanks to the intoxication produced by the mouth-watering dishes, the hanriya, Bhauji's laughter and her melodious song that I got up late the next morning. A large crowd had gathered at the door. It turned out that Lalchan Da and his Baba had gone to the akhra. The akhra was a community space where the elders and the wise men of the village sat together every Thursday to resolve any local problems. On the festival days of Sarhul, Hariyari and Sohrai, the maandar would beat there the whole night. The young men of the village would gather for the night, and the young girls would come too. The moon would skip to the tunes of Jhoomar and Jadura all night. The sakhua and the palaash trees would join the ballet. The kaner and the amaltas would dance a waltz. The rivers, cataracts and hills would dance, all of nature swept up in the music.

But that day was neither a festival day, nor was it Thursday or Friday. The crowd looked angry. The light-hearted feeling of the festivals was absent. I reckoned Ramchan had created some problem. He had been married off quite early to curb his noxious habits, but he had not reformed. The mates and the munshis of the mines on the paat were outsiders, and none of them had brought their families here. They asked for Asur girls only to do their household work. Why? It was anyone's guess. One could easily spot two or three Asur girls working at their houses. In no time at all, they, too, turned into fallen women, like Ramrati in the town. The mine officials used spoiled youths like Ramchan as their pimps. Lalchan Da and Baba used to receive such complaints frequently.

But I was wrong. Today's crowd had not arrived with a grievance against Ramchan. It was one of the village boys, Soma, who had a gripe against his own Baba. The matter, more or less, was that his Baba had handed over one acre of land to a quarry owner's middleman in return for a measly five thousand rupees. He had put his thumb print on a blank piece of paper without considering the young son's future or consulting his family. Why? And it was not only Soma's Baba. Everybody was falling for the honey trap of these sly men.

The attitude of all the mine owners, big or small, was similar. They preferred mining on the gair-majurwa and Asur raiyat land, rather than the land leased out to them. Illegal mining had been rampant for years. Rumjhum and Lalchan Da's awareness campaign and the numerous applications to the district collector and the superintendent of police (SP) had proved futile. Once Rumjhum and Lalchan conducted a comprehensive survey to note down the mouja, khata, plot and raqba numbers of the pieces of land that had fallen to illegal mining, as well as the registration numbers of the trucks that transported the bauxite from the mines, finally drafting an application running ten to fifteen pages and handing it over personally to the collector in his office. Later, they were told that the task of the official enquiry had been deputed to the district mining officer. The cat was now the minder of the milk! Naturally, nothing happened. However, Shindalco company fixed vapour lamps on all the electric poles in the Magistrates' Colony and took on their maintenance. The upkeep and expenditure of one of the parks in the colony was now shifted to the care of the company gardener. This was the only follow up to the fifteen-page application. Eventually, a few more conscious people like Lalchan Da and Rumjhum began exerting social pressure to make sure that nobody would give his raiyati land to the companies. If they did, there would be no land left to plant one's foot on for inhabitation, let alone for cultivation. Where would the Asurs go, then?

But this morning, Soma's Baba seemed to have gone deaf and dumb. He did not reply to a single question. For all he cared, everyone could go on banging their heads against the wall.

The hours passed. The sun rose high. Everybody had to look after their own work. Finally, Lalchan's Baba got up and led the old man aside, taking him to one end of the akhra. Suddenly, Soma's Baba broke into a loud wail. Everyone in the akhra froze. Lalchan's Baba returned to whisper something in his son's ears. Lalchan whispered in turn into Rumjhum's ears. Gradually, the news spread through the whole akhra. People bowed their heads and started leaving, one by one, taking heavy steps. The story was that Soma's sister, who had been married off in a distant village, had contracted cerebral malaria two or three days ago. Her in-laws had taken her to a private clinic in the city. The doctors did their best but she had not survived. The private clinic refused to hand over the body without receiving the money for her treatment. The son-in-law arranged for some money and, broken, had come to Soma's Baba for help. The dead body of the daughter had to be brought back home, so the old man had hardly had a choice.

6

Like its deity, Sing-Bonga, the primitive Asur community never tired. Born from fire, once an iron-smelting people fed on molten steel, they too, had turned into steel. It is difficult to believe that men can labour so hard on the paltry sustenance offered by maize and roots. The fertile land on the paat also looked rock-barren in the absence of water. The Asurs continued to be absorbed in preparing the land for cultivation, digging and ploughing it without pause before every rainy season.

The work in the mines was no less rigorous. Buoyed by the elixir of toil, hopping through Jadura, Jhoomar and Karam dance steps during the Sarhul, Hariyari, Sohrai and Sadasi-Kutasi festivals and celebrations, the Asurs led a communal existence with their baiga-pujar-pahan, and continued hustling on their winged steeds of life.

My year here passed swiftly. The maize in kharif, a little paddy, and sarguja and urad pulses in rabi. The crops covered the dusty paat with a green veil. The tiny, sunflower-like blossoms of sarguja transfigured the horizon. The earth began to look like a shy, smiling bride draped in a golden chunar. Sometimes, it seemed as though the rays of Sing-Bonga, and Sun God himself, had transformed into oil-bearing buds. The surroundings seemed to be swinging in a cape of the yellow flowers, swathed in the smile and hum of Mother Earth.

The baigas, pujars and the pahan calculated the movements of the stars and the planets to propitiate worship at the Sarna. The paat's deity, Sarna Mai, the All-compassionate Mahadeva and Sing-Bonga, would then be pleased with the village. The objective of each such ceremony was to ensure the welfare of the farms and barnyards, the cattle and the kine, the children and the toddlers, the family and the locality. The village could sleep peacefully only after it had propitiated the reigning divinity of the locality and its pastoral threshold.

In addition to this, the people always recalled their forefathers with deference. During the naming ceremony of a new-born child, the villagers not only remembered their ancestors but also believed their spirits were present on the occasion. Two grains of rice were put in water in a leaf cup in the memory of each ancestor. If the grains sank to the bottom, it was thought that the particular ancestor was not willing to let the child be named after him. But if the grains kept floating and if their ends came together, it was assumed that this ancestor was willing and the child would be named after him.

Sing-Bonga seemed fed up those summer days, glaring down angrily with red eyes. The showers in the month of Asharh beckoned to the people to begin preparations for the kharif crops, and the villagers became occupied with that. The days of hospitality were over. Now was the time for back-breaking work. Even habitual wanderers like Lalchan Da and Rumjhum became rare sights. I had to pass my free hours at Doctor Ram Kumar's or at Budhani Di's shop in Sakhuapaat.

Budhani came from the community of Melan Asur, the bhabho of the headmaster, the wife of his younger brother. Melan Headmaster was the first person with an MA from the primitive Asur tribe. He was posted at a boarding school nearly 40 kilometres from Sakhuapaat, but his family was still here. His younger brother, Budhani's husband, was feeble-minded and a dimwit. The headmaster's gomkain was an utterly simple housewife. The meek woman was always busy with household work. The headmaster did not have much arable land. Since single man's income was not sufficient for the extended family, Budhani had left for Assam with her children and husband nearly five years earlier. She undertook various jobs there. And then maybe at Dibrugarh, or at Sibsagar, her tea stall had struck gold. She had employed a number of boys from Bihar and Bengal as helping hands and learnt to prepare a variety of delicacies from them. The Jharkhandi dhuska with ghughuni, idlis, Bihari gulgula, piyazi, kachari, sev-bundiya were the snacks she usually offered with tea. Her sweet voice, fastidiousness in hygiene and her irresistible, beautiful face pulled large crowds to her shop.

Things were going fine until one gloomy morning, when the Hindi-speaking people were declared outsiders. Bullets rained on the tea-garden colonies at night, changing them to murky, fuming rivers of coal and tar. Soon enough, the corpses of the young men and women began to bob like logs in the hot, boiling surge of the coal tar. It was a night without a morning. The sun, too, seemed to smear coal tar on its face and run into hiding.

Budhani abandoned everything to undertake a seven-day journey back to Sakhuapaat, her husband and children in tow. She did not lose her wits during the terrible violence, and collected her savings passbooks along with the jewellery and the cash she had stashed at home. Her money was transferred to the Koelbigha Block State Bank through the efforts of Melan Headmaster Sahib, Ram Kumar, and with the help of the bank manager, Kujur Sahib. Budhani overcame all hurdles and set up shop at Sakhuapaat. She shook off her fatigue and worries and stood proud once more. After all, she was an Asur siyani! The molten iron swigged by her forefathers coursed through her veins too.

However, at first, hardly anyone preferred her shop to Singhji's more famous one.

'What does an Asurin know about cooking dhuska and gulgula?'

'These people are always filthy; who would want to touch anything cooked by her?'

Singhji's propaganda machine worked overtime. The richer one is, the more one hankers after money. Singhji was not satisfied with his earnings from the jam-packed hotel, taken from the pockets of truck drivers and cleaners, the shopkeepers from the market and the mining office employees. As soon as dusk fell, his clandestine sale of hanriya and wine took off. Singhji would also reap huge profits from the supply of labourers after the kharif harvest.

'The Singhjiyawa was a lot more interested in supplying girls and women,' Lalchan told me. 'His pimps would snoop through every household. They would mislead young girls at an impressionable age, luring them with glamorous stories of Delhi and Kolkata. If a wife was not happy with her husband, they would brainwash her. The market would be bustling with such pimps after the kharif harvest.

'One of the five girls from Lodhma below was a dropout from class eight. She somehow managed to send out a postcard. When the postman put the letter in Doctor Sahib's hands on market day, we realized the tortures our daughters suffer. Only God knows which massage parlour mistress they had been auctioned off to!

'A case was registered at the police station. When we staged a sit-down before the SP's office, raids were conducted in Delhi. Our daughters were returned to us. Only then was the mischief of Singhjiyawa brought to light. The testimony of the girls landed Singhji and his sons and sires in jail.'

Maybe nothing stays hidden from the eyes of the paat deity, Sarna Mai, Sing-Bonga and the All-compassionate Mahadeva. A padlock soon dangled from the door of Singhji's hotel. Naturally, all his former customers made a beeline to Budhani's shop. And they were captivated by the flavour of Budhani's 'pecial chai' (special tea) soon enough.

'And we had never tasted such mouth-watering dhuska, kachari, piyazi and bundiya until today!'

The goodwill made the whole Sakhuapaat market flock to Budhani's tea stall. She subscribed to two newspapers. The radio blared out the news at full volume. Cleanliness and sweet words reigned. The stall was always chock-a-block with customers.

I purchased a pair of canvas shoes at the local market. Before sunrise, I would jog 4 kilometres from Bhaunrapaat to Sakhuapaat to sip Budhani Di's tea. Then, if I felt like it, I would walk back or flag down a bauxite truck to hitch a ride. The exercise kept me fresh for the whole day.

At first, Etwari sulked. 'What's this? Going so far to simply have tea?'

She remained sullen for a couple of days but eventually accepted my routine. She had begun to assert herself with me in this fashion and I relished it.

One morning, I heard that Lalchan Da's uncle had been sacrificed at the Ambatoli Devi Thaan. His head had been found lying there.

7

I handed my leave application to Etwari and pedalled off on the bicycle, reaching Ambatoli with the swiftness of a tempest. The house was deserted. The family had rushed down to Mahua Toli. The road through the woods and the hills was unfamiliar to me, so I found a boy from the tola to lead me there. It took me the better part of an hour to reach.

The severed head had been found at Devi Thaan. The torso had been carried on a string cot from the don field. The police force from the Koelbigha station was already there. There was a whisper that this had been the handiwork of Gonu Singh's family. He had had his greedy eyes on the five-acre, rice-bearing don land and had often tried to pressure the family into selling it to him. The fields adjoining Lalchan Da's had slowly been manipulated and come under Gonu's proprietorship. The entire district knew of how this vicious family had come to own the hundred-acre don fields, slowly expanding from their paltry three-acre taand. But nobody had the nerve to oppose them for fear of the malicious, extended clan and reprisal from the sons, nephews and sons-in-law. Whenever this family sought help, the members of the Kanari Babuani family supported them with their fierce might. There was an undercurrent of terror, and all rumours of their wrongdoing were suppressed. The FIR in this particular case mentioned 'unknown assailants'. The cronies of this nasty gang, posing as well-wishers, put up an impressive show of helping the aggrieved household. They not only arranged for the string cot but also for a tractor to take the body for the post-mortem. Lalchan Da and his paternal cousin went along to the mortuary. The rest of the crowd began the climb back up the hill, their steps leaden.

I returned to my room after an hour and a half, Rumjhum in tow. Food had been kept for me, but I felt neither like going to school nor eating. Etwari peeped in after some time. She sensed my mood when she saw the untouched food. She was also quite sad at the news, and her eyes were brimming with tears. She handed me a cup of tea silently. I had no choice but to accept it.

I could understand what Rumjhum must be feeling. We avoided each other's eyes. It was not only this murder; this was not the first nor would it be the last assault on an Asur. It was not even the first killing for land. It was simply the latest happening in the overt, and often covert, strife that had been going on for thousands of years. The severed head baffled my perception of time and space. I was confused—were we living in the Vedic Age or the twenty-first century? The present dissolved into the past as the mindless massacres of yesteryears whirled before my eyes. What was it that had changed a community into the 'other', made them 'different', an enemy? Was it simply because their lifestyle was different from ours that they had become objects of abuse and butchery? Why did some of us take the discovery of fire and metals, and the art of smelting ores in such a bad spirit that this race of artisans had had to face continual assaults and retreats?

I was reminded of the Incas, Mayans, Aztecs and the hundreds of Native Americans from Western history. They, too, had been driven away and decimated in a similar fashion. Like them, only a handful of the Asurs survived, leading a wretched life sans culture, sans language, sans literature, sans religion. Perhaps mainstream civilization had persuaded itself of the need to consume them utterly. The Americans were generous enough to preserve the literatures and ruins of the Incas, the Mayans, the Aztecs and the Native Americans in a number of museums. But the self-proclaimed liberal and tolerant Indian culture had spared not even that much space for the Asurs. They existed only as vestiges of myths. They had no literature, no history, and no museum, and were not accorded even the faintest sign of their devastation.

Now and then, some eccentric anthropologist or archaeologist would suggest that the local legends hinted at the remains of Asur mud forts at Dhasi, 24 kilometres from Azamgarh. In Azamgarh, the ruins on the banks of the Kunwar and Mungi rivers were claimed to belong to the Asurs.

The legend was that a powerful king, Banasur, extended his reign over a large part of North India, up to Assam and north Bengal. Several places were named after him, most notably, baked brick ruins. The stories told in a village called Masarh in Shahabad spoke of Banasur and the marriage of his daughter Usha to Lord Krishna's grandson. The pond at the northern end of Banasur's palace is still called by his name.

It was also said that the Bakri village, 3 kilometres from Ara, was founded by Bakasur. His battle with the Pandavas dominated the legends of the area. Gaya lay ahead, founded by the Asur, Gayasur. The distinguished king of Magadh, Jarasandh, was probably the most famous of the emperors from the Asur dynasty, and Rajgriha was his capital. The ancient but excellent road from Nawada to Rajgir through Sidhaul village was known as Asurin. It implied an aeons-long withdrawal, leading finally to this paat. The end of the earth. Where would this people go now? The juggernaut of annihilation ground on. The lands and the daughters submitted silently, mute, being deprived of their legacy, piece by piece.

Was it Rumjhum speaking? I merely sensed his words. Some felt, some heard, some spoken, all droning on in the silence. I heard the sobs of a vanquished race jolting the portals of time, beyond the pages of history.

8

People routinely entered into hair-splitting discussions and anxious attempts to discover the true roots of Gonu alias Ganeshwar Singh. Was he Rajput or Kherwar? He claimed the Rajput status. He had married his daughters into Rajput families from the neighbouring districts. But the sons and the nephews could not be wedded into Rajput lineage. Nobody was inclined to confirm the reason. Who would dare ask? It was like belling the cat.

The elders said that Gonu's father had once been the most dreaded dacoit in the locality. Six-and-a-half feet tall and pitch black in complexion, he had towered over everyone. His partner, equally gigantic, had been an Oraon from the Dombatoli. But the two had a soft corner for their native village and the neighbouring areas. They never committed any theft, robbery, snatching or murder here.

They would take to their dark trade during the rainy season or just after. The Koel river would be in torrential spate, spilling from bank to bank. There was no bridge or a boat over it. The robust pair would swim through the violent flow, confident of their prowess, tying the gold, jewellery and money in a towel and wearing it like a turban on their heads. The police chased them but could get no further than the river bank. They would wring their hands helplessly when the two jumped into its currents. The Koel was witness to many such chases, but the outside world never got the slightest whiff of them.

Gonu's father had converted the three-acre taand into 30 acres of don with his earnings from these robberies, and it was Gonu's turn now. He transformed the face of robbery. His high school education came in handy. There were plenty of perks from accompanying the MLA to the block office, the police station and the district courts. He used his brains instead of brawn.

First of all, he placed his village home in the care of his elder brother and built himself a house at a spot in the Koelbigha market taand. From its veranda, he could keep an eye on the thana, the hospital and the block office, all while lounging in his chair.

The frequent visits to the block office acquainted him with the tricks needed to wrangle government projects. Now he had become so cocky that when his son Rajendra Singh, nephew Virendra Singh, son-in-law Prakash Singh, his son-in-law's brother Ayodhya Singh and his own Bullet motorcycle appeared at the block office, the sternest of the officers would blanch in fear. Nobody but the Gonu clan could imagine touching a contract from any of the government departments in the panchayats north of the Koel River.

By the time Gonu turned fifty, he had extended the 30-acre don inherited from his father to 50 acres. But the detractors said that he had had twenty acres to his name by claiming to be a member of the Kherwar tribe. Naturally, people enquired whether he was a Kherwar or a Rajput. But who had the cheek to ask him? Even a child in his family peed fire. There was a saying in the area that if a man rises, he turns Rajput, and if he falls, he becomes a Kherwar. The implication is that if a Kherwar grows prosperous, he acquires the stature of a Rajput and if he falls upon bad days, he becomes a simple Kherwar tribal.

Gonu Singh had to hand out three to four dozen sarees every festival day. He was hard put to remember how many mistresses he had in the various villages and from varying castes. So, when many of his alleged consorts, some of whom had begun to look older than him, came down on Holi or Diwali to receive the gifts, he was unable to recognize them. Since his grandchildren were now growing up, it was all rather embarrassing.

But Gonuwa was Gonuwa, a real son of a wicked father. It was not that he had turned religious in his old age. He would exploit the young daughters of his mistresses shrewdly—calculating who was to seduce the Bara Babu of the thana, who was to be reserved for BDO Sahib, the block development officer, and which of them would massage the MLA's legs during his night stay. The old fellow was foxy in his cunning.

There was a small story behind the night stay. It was said that Gonu had acquired a fondness for English during his visits to the officers of the block. He would ram in an English word or two now and then. Once, the MLA came down to visit to the block. Gonu was hovering around him. Evening had fallen, so he asked him to defer his departure till the morning. To impress the officers, he requested the MLA, 'Huzoor! Have nightfall here tonight.' He used 'nightfall' instead of 'night stay.' The arrow had been shot. For a moment, everyone was stunned by Gonu Singh's blunder. But the very next instant they realized his mistake and broke into guffaws. Gonu gaped foolishly.

The black dye of black money now ran in his veins. Its dark shadow had not spared his house. The family had faced that darkness a number of times, but the foolishness of wealth overshadowed all their thinking. People said that one of Gonu's sisters, who had been thrown out by her husband, had settled down in her brother's house. She had a sharp tongue. Gonu's wife was sick of her sour comments and taunts. One day, when everyone was at the haat, the house was deserted. The sister-in-law had stayed behind because she was not feeling well. Gonu's wife finished her off with one blow from the axe and concealed the corpse in the dung heap in a corner of the courtyard. She feigned ignorance when the search for the woman began that night. The matter was discovered only when the stench became unbearable. People were suspicious, but there had been no eyewitnesses. Naturally, nobody could point a finger at her. The waves of the Koel River once again engulfed the gossip so neatly that the news never made it to the taand police station.

Let alone the other members of the household, Gonu Singh himself was afraid of his wife. A few years later, when a young, youthful niece vanished without a trace, Gonu and the brothers took a brutal decision. One night, he hacked his own wife into tiny bits and sank them in the Koel.

The Gonu Singh clan did not lack for wealth or land but their hunger continued to grow. They'd had their eyes on Lalchan Da's family's paddy field for years. That morning, Uncle had gone to harrow it before the sowing began. It had probably still been dark. Since the place was deserted, the killer must have carried out his task expertly and leisurely. He had to have been vicious enough to take the severed head three quarters of a mile, from the field to the Devi Thaan as an offering. Virgin paddy, grass leaves, the earthen lamp and wick, sindoor, leaves from the mango tree—everything had been arranged for the homage.

I could not get the chopped head out of my mind. My eating went awry. I would wake up with a start in the middle of the night. Finally, Rumjhum brought me a book on the decimation of the native peoples of America. It told the story of Metacom, the king of Massachusetts.

In 1620 AD, an English ship dropped anchor at Cape Cod in Massachusetts. More than half the passengers had perished when the ship was caught in a snowstorm. Those who made it were in a pitiable state. They survived only on whatever they could scrounge from the sea. They were swinging between life and death when a native, Samoset, took them to the chief of his community, Massasoit. King Massasoit provided them shelter and sent them maize; the king and his men saved the Englishmen from cold and hunger.

King Massasoit died in 1661 and his son, Metacom, was elected chief. By this time, hundreds of thousands of the English had arrived. Unable to comprehend the concept of communal ownership, they ignored the rights of the native community and embarked on a relentless campaign to grab their land.

King Metacom foresaw the danger. He contacted all the other tribes of Massachusetts and invited them to a communal dance to forge unity. The celebration continued for days. The English took the dance as a declaration of war; perhaps they felt threatened. They launched an attack on the natives. The attack resulted in a bloody massacre. King Metacom was arrested, along with his wife and children. Paying no heed to the kindness they had been shown earlier, the heartless Englishmen enslaved the family and sent them to the Bermuda jungles as manual labour, along with African slaves. The king was beheaded without a formal trial, and his scalp was hung in a public place where it dangled for twenty years to generate fear among the tribesmen.

The severed heads of Uncle and Metacom merged in my mind. I was perplexed, confused once again. Where was I? What age was this?

9

The Asurin has gone to sell wood,
Has gone to sell the bamboo.
She has a fancy for the Mate
She is coy with the Munshi
For lucre's sake she has ruined her family
For money's sake she has stained her caste.

Young men often sang this song about the Asur girls. The lifestyle of the Asur girls who worked in the houses of the mine mates, munshis, clerks and officers altered quickly. They would doll themselves up with snow-powder, face paint, alta and fake jewellery. Ramrati, the mistress of Ansari, the contractor of Sakhuapaat, was not the only one of her kind. The contamination was spreading through the paat like an infectious disease. I felt the song was some sort of censor. The community was cautioning them—you are treading the wrong path, take care.

However, Rumjhum told me it was not so much a complaint as a wail—the wailing of a community as it disintegrated. Hunger and poverty had hollowed their lives so badly that the social system had collapsed. The opinions of the baigas, pahans and pujars and the elders of the village were being taken more lightly every day. If the food in the house was barely enough for three or four months' survival, who could stop the sons from leaving the village and the daughters from turning into concubines in outsiders' homes?

Budhani Di made exclusive sitting arrangements for us at her tea stall. A thatch roof panel was tilted against the wall and covered with bamboo slats on two sides. And so the desi cabin was ready! After Uncle's murder, a group of youths from the Asur community would gather to exchange views with Lalchan Da and Rumjhum. Barely any of them were graduates, but the number of matriculate boys was large. The only postgraduate in the tribe was Melan Headmaster. One or two of them were studying for their MA degrees. One was Lalita, Lalchan's niece, the daughter of his elder brother. She was doing a post-graduation course in history. Rumjhum's younger brother, Sunil, was a year senior to her and wanted to break the university record for his favourite subject, mathematics.

In Budhani Di's desi cabin, we heard that the Gonu clan would begin sowing Uncle's field on the next full moon night. Men were being called in from all around. Invitations had also been sent to the Kanari Babuanis. The sister of Gonu Singh's son-in-law had been married into the richest family of Babuani Toli. They, too, intended to come to Mahua Toli to fulfil their kinship obligations.

Lalchan Da decided we would sow the seedlings that very night. Everyone realized the consequences of being dispossessed of land. There was no time to be lost in talk and gossip. No fewer than sixty burly young men like Balchan had to be chosen and brought together from the paat. The supply of seedlings was no problem. The real difficulty was finding muzzle-loaders and kattas, the locally made pistols. The total number of licensed guns and rifles in Mahua Toli and Babuani Toli was no more than ten or twelve, but there was no shortage of illegal arms. The larger the number of bows and arrows and hatchets, the better it would be.

I felt that if there were to be a fight with the Babuani, our relations with Doctor Sahib Ram Kumar would be strained. Upset, Rumjhum scolded me, saying that I should not speak without full knowledge of the facts. I had hardly been a season on the paat, he pointed out. What did I know about Doctor Sahib? His relations with the Babuanis were as bad as ours, supposedly.

I still did not understand anything but the worm of my doubt vanished. Lalchan Da told me, 'You should not follow us tonight. Don't even leave the paat. If possible, arrange for the truck of one of the Asur drivers to wait near Mahua Toli on the foot trail, in the shadows. Etwa Asur would be the best choice. He does not drink or loaf.

He can stay awake all night. Etwari knows him well. Send a message.'

Doctor Ram Kumar did not have to go back to Kanari that night. His task, if he could do it, was to arrange first aid. It was certain that a clash would take place during the sowing. People knew the Gonu family too well.

As night fell, a group of about seventy youths reached the field. It was around ten or eleven at night. Balchan was in the lead. Lalchan had been asked to stay behind. They moved so stealthily that not even the dry leaves on the jungle floor were rustled. Etwari, a drunk Gandoor, Lalchan's Baba and Ayo, his sister-in-law and other women and elders of the tola, sat on the wooded incline, a little below the paat, keeping their ears pricked, to hear the sounds coming from Mahua Toli. I asked Etwa to stop the truck and came to the spot as well.

Later on, Rumjhum told me that the sowing business had proceeded quite smoothly for three hours. Half of the work was done when a roar rose from Mahua Toli. The splashing of the water in the field revealed that somebody had been keeping watch from the trees. Gonu's nephew Virendra Singh may have been the first to arrive. He had a sword in hand and a katta tucked in at his waist. As he advanced, swishing his sword, full of abuse, Balchan held him by his wrists and throat. He lifted the buffalo-like man into the air and threw him against his own motorcycle. His spine broke. He fell down thrashing, never to get up again.

But within minutes, a crowd of hundreds surrounded the planters and began advancing towards them. The defenders' arrows stalled them for a while but eventually, the attackers' rifles began to dominate. Muzzle-loaders, kattas, bows and arrows were unable to stop them. It was their haunt, so they had the upper hand. Our men held on until Balchan was shot and wounded. When he fell, they retreated discreetly. After the climb up the slope, we found out that seven people had been hurt. Four of them, including Balchan, had injuries from bullets. Three had been struck by swords and lathis. Balchan fared the worst among the injured. He was so drenched in blood that it was hard to locate the bullet wound.

Etwa sped off in his truck and we reached Sakhuapaat in no time. Doctor Sahib was not only up, he had also summoned the staff of the primary health centre. They were playing cards to fight off sleep. Shallow cuts and scratches were not much to be concerned about, and these were dressed quickly. The real worry was for the bullet victims. The buck shots were extracted painstakingly. But Balchan had taken bullets in the stomach as well as the thigh. Soma had also been hit; the bullet had gone in just below his rib cage. Ram Kumar tried to stop the bleeding with injections and bandages. Etwa gunned his truck again. The health centre staff went with Lalchan and Rumjhum to the Sadar Hospital.

The other injured men were cured in a matter of days,

but Balchan's stomach wound refused to heal. It filled up with pus over and over again. Doctor Sahib changed the dressing regularly, and a variety of costly medicines were administered, but the wound remained green. Finally, Ram Kumar took Balchan to the most renowned physician in the state capital. It was revealed that the antibiotic he had been using was spurious. The genuine one was bought and things improved after that.

Balchan's fall had shaken Lalchan Da badly. The fire seemed to have gone out of his voice. But his lack of enthusiasm was made up for by Rumjhum's passionate involvement.

The question persisted. This issue had dogged them for thousands of years. It was an eternal, primeval doubt, and no one had found the answer, neither their forefathers nor they themselves. How long could the Asurs run, to which point? And from this paat, where would they go?

10

One morning, Rumjhum brought me a book on the Sing-Bonga legend of the Mundas. Chuckling, he told me that it never matters who emerges victorious, because he nurtures only one feeling towards the vanquished—hatred. 'He who is more violent, more barbaric and better trained in the art of killing triumphs; only he who possesses mightier weapons that can pluck away the best blossom of creation, man. Truth and honesty do not win in a war, contrary to what is said in stories. These tales of truth and honesty are put together by pandering poets. We accept the stories of these bootlickers and yarn-spinning toadies blindly. The power of their pens is employed in attesting that the vanquished race was dishonest, unjust and unfair, all in an attempt to wash off the consciousness of guilt rising from the blood-soaked earth, women, wealth and the crown. You will realize it once you finish the book.'

The sum total of the long Mundari ballad was that groups of Asur brethren, in bunches, like bananas, were unceasingly blowing air into their hearths in eighty-one fields and eighty-three taands. They were smelting non-stop, causing a storm to blow in the sky and a fog to form on the earth. The flora and the fauna wilted in the heat. Insects and bugs, creepy-crawlies, were perishing, one by one. The lotus-bearing ponds and the pools where the lilies grew were drying up. The Munda people had been thrashing in thirst and hunger for seven days and seven nights, just like the birds. Even Lord Sing-Bonga and Goddess Kumari were disconcerted by the acrid, smoke-filled sky.

Lord Sing-Bonga sent bird after bird as messengers to the Asurs, to ask them to stop the bellows. But the rock-chested and arkanthe-armed Asur did not give a hoot for the warnings. They considered themselves no less than the gods. They tortured the birds. They held them in tongs and pounded them with the hammer. Burning coal was showered on some, hot ashes on others.

Finally, in order to punish the arrogant, wicked Asurs, Lord Sing-Bonga transformed himself into a boy suffering from a skin disease, He began serving at the house of the Lutkum Old Man and Old Woman. While he was working there, He killed the Asurs greedy for gold and silver by charring them in their own furnaces. When He was returning to the sky, the Asur women hung from his feet. Then Lord Sing-Bonga jerked his legs so violently that they were knocked down into the hills, woods, waterfalls and streams. They turned into ghosts.

Rumjhum believed that the narrative presented a small glimpse of the story of the destruction of their race. They had retreated from the Sapta Sindhu region in the Vedic Age, through Azamgarh, Shahabad, Ara, Gaya and Rajgir to the forested Kikat, Paundrik, Kokrah or Chutiya Nagpur areas. Nobody had reckoned in the annals how many times and how many Indras, Pandavas and Sing-Bongas had destroyed them over those thousands of years. They survived only in folktales and myths.

Anthropologists contended that in the Khunti town, there were over thirty-three sites showing signs of the Asur civilization. These included the evidence of their iron smelting, remnants of baked brick dwellings and burial grounds. Many of the mounds were still known as Asurgarhs. The waves of Munda invaders, followed by Oraons, had pushed and chased them to their current homes, to the paat on the hills. This barren, flat plateau had sheltered them in its lap. But in the census, their number was only eight or nine thousand; were they really so meagre a community? Or was it the continual decimation after each defeat and obliteration of their best warriors, sages, apothecaries and teachers that had led to their population becoming so paltry?

We can only imagine the terrible consequences of the unrelenting pursuit of the Asur race.

Rumjhum referred to the chapter on the 'Trail of Tears' in the book about the Native Americans. Maybe reading that could give me an idea of the destruction of the Asur community too.

The deluge of Europeans, greedy for gold mines, pushed the natives back time and again. The imperialistic powers were advancing, following the policy of gaining control of land by hook or by crook. No documents before 1633 exist to validate any suspicious land deal. In several instances, land was grabbed by duping tribal chiefs by offering them paltry gifts or medals. False treaties and the exchange of fake documents became a tactic in many cases. Might was used where other ploys failed. It was during the course of the resistance that the Cherokee Battle (1759–61) and the Ottawa Uprising (1763) took place, under Chief Pontiac's leadership.

The colonial powers aimed at expansion to take over the cotton-growing land. During the presidencies of Thomas Jefferson and James Madison, fifty-three treaties were forced on the Native Americans to seize their land. The imperialists dishonoured those same treaties every time and encroachment never ceased. To protect themselves, the chief of the Shawnee tribe, Tecumseh and his brother Frofet, formed a confederation of Native Americans in 1811. But they lost the Tippenkoy Battle.

Finally, the land-grabbing campaign was declared a state policy in the second decade of the eighteenth century. President James Monroe floated an official proposal that stated that the Indians of the South Confederation would have to vacate their land and settle in the region west of the Mississippi. However, the Cherokee tribal federation framed its own constitution in 1828 and declared sovereignty. The American Supreme Court upheld their right to own land. President Andrew Jackson did not concur with the decision of the Supreme Court. He enacted the Indian Removal Bill in 1830. Budgetary allocations were made to displace them. In 1837, fourteen thousand Indians were dislocated. Between 1835 and 1840, six hundred million dollars were spent on uprooting the Seminole tribe. Sixteen thousand Cherokee tribals were besieged, in their tepees, by the army. After that summer, they were dispatched, during the rainy season, on a 1500-kilometre journey. Their possessions were bundled onto wooden carts. Around eight thousand children, women, old people and the sick died in the course of the evacuation. A few years later, in 1841, forty-eight pony-drawn carts carrying skeletons reached Sacramento on the infamous Oregon Trail. The tragic passage is called the Trail of Tears.

We were at a loss for words after going through the horrible descriptions. The evening seemed to grow heavy. Sing-Bonga was uneasy too, it seemed, and covered His face.

11

Time moves so swiftly that one errand or another always remains unfinished. When I went back to my native place during the vacation, everything seemed strange and unfamiliar. The greenery here was not as bright and profound as it seemed in the paat. There was no brilliant ruby palaash, no fragrance of gulainchi, no cream and jade blossoms of sakhua or the exciting drip of the mahua. The river did not flow, trilling, as the hilly paat brook did, nor did it have the same coolness. The village seemed inferior in many ways. Here was no darkish Etwari, or the taste of her tomato-garlic garnished koynaar saag. Neither was there Madam Minj, Kachchap Madam, Sushma Singh Kherwar or the little girls' chorus, which would soothe me to sleep like a lullaby and wake me up like the morning prayer. Here was no 'pecial chai' made by Budhani or the sharp, hot taste of dhuska and ghughuni. I also missed the brother-in-law song, Lalchan Bhauji's smile, Ram Kumar Doctor's ingenious ideas and the books in the school library.

I had never imagined I would grow so fond of the paat so far from my native place. I now laughed and felt embarrassed, recalling my early efforts at getting a transfer. However, my father and my uncle often tried to convince me that it had been a long time, and we should visit Samdhiji once again. I would change the topic and postpone matters. My strongest, most sturdy defence was that my sister's marriage negotiations should have first priority.

My dreams were filled either with the ringing words of Lalchan Da or rising and receding purple waves. The captivating magic of this particular colour was overwhelming. The school campus, the classrooms, the library and the teachers' quarters, everything was daubed with it. Translucent, lavender brilliance kept pouring over me. The charm must have been cast on that moonlit night when Gandoor, Jamunia and I had sat down to enjoy a drink. The moon, too, dropped by to give us company. We poured a drink into a leaf cup for him but he was not able to finish it. The laughter of the moonlight transformed into dew drops that dripped into the cup. I listened to the breath-taking choir of the moonlight, absorbing the purple glow and the smell of the gulainchi blossom, the jaggery-sweet chuan on the Phuljhar Hill, from which water trickled ever so sluggishly. Jamunia, the moonlight and the gulainchi whispered their longing to go to the dugout with their lovers and fill their vessels:

At Phuljhar Hill, the jaggery-sweet dugout,
And the water seeping out languorous
Oozing languorous
Water seeping, pure water
I will collect it with my beau
With my gold-like mate
The seeping water
Oozing
At Phuljhar Hill…

The melody fell over me. The song was being hummed and heard not only by Jamunia, the moonlight and gulainchi but by the wide paat too. Maybe it was the magical song or the heady hanriya liquor that led to Gandoor gradually reclining on the grass. The jealous gulainchi began dropping sweet blossoms over him. This was the break Jamunia had been waiting for. She stretched out her hand and a dense swathe of clouds covered the moon's eyes. A tide swelled in the wilderness and the purple hue swamped me. I kept bobbing in the surge and the dusky wash tinted me from head to toe.

My dyed existence took me beyond the banal accounts of worldly profit and loss. But Jamunia's habit of bossing over me had begun to annoy me. She decided the colour of my shirts, the hour for washing the bed sheets, the shade of the curtains, my destinations, my schedule and who I should be friends with. Jamunia wanted to resolve everything. I put up a show of irritation but in my core, a spring of elixir began to flow. The jaggery-sweet dugout of Phuljhar Hill came alive in the dry desert of my heart.

One fine morning, we heard at Budhani Di's desi cabin that the Gonu clan had pulled out the seedlings we had planted in Uncle's rice-producing don and re-sown the field. It was a case of forcible possession. People became fidgety. Rumjhum, Soma, Bhikha—everyone was in a mood to teach them a lesson with some help from the Jungle Party. Anger and agitation had forced them to take such a desperate step. Balchan had still not recovered from his injuries. The bullet shot that bloody night had broken his spirit. However, Lalchan Da did not agree to the proposed plans, and Rumjhum's anger ballooned. I called Doctor Sahib when tempers began to fray.

The arguments stopped when he entered. In Doctor Sahib's opinion, the battle could not be won if we fought alone. It was not merely the issue of Lalchan Da's five acres; other matters had to be taken up to make the operation successful. Every day, a charade would take place on the paat. A number of Asurs were misled and made to agree to illegal mining. Land was snatched away from them by cheating them in every way possible. Bauxite was taken out to leave behind gulfs of death. If all the issues were joined and brought up together, the Asurs, Oraons, Kherwars and Sadaans would unite. The bottom line was that they could not counter the lathis of the ruthless, barbaric Gonu clan alone.

The Gonu clan threw its weight around everywhere, be it the police station or the court. We were left with no option but to involve the fellows from Kanari Navayuvak Samgha. Boys like Madan, Shyam, James and Philip had put a check on Babuani bullying in Kanari haat. It had not been a simple fight. The Babuanis had been a terror in the market for decades. They laid claim to everything they liked in the haat—chickens, goats, young daughters or daughters-in-law. A number of scuffles had taken place because of this. Thana police, court, jail, they had manipulated everyone. But the Kanari Navayuwak Samgha never buckled or gave in. They would now help us in our battle.

It was remarkably true. The long, drawn-out feud could be fought with the help of Navayuwak Samgha and possibly, won. Ram Kumar was right when he told us that every Thursday, only two matters came up in the akhra—that this fellow had put his thumb impression on a blank piece of paper given by the mine middleman, or that fellow's daughter had left home for good or was still living on the paat in the household of the mates and the munshis and refused to come home. Poverty, hunger and disease shattered their every hope.

It was finally decided that, at dawn, Rumjhum would visit Kanari in secret. James Lakra was his college mate. It would be better if Soma and Bhikha went along with Rumjhum.

Old doubts reared their heads again. Why was Doctor Ram Kumar playing the role of Vibhishan? He belonged to Babuanis but never seemed to take their side. I didn't know whom to turn to. I did not want to be chided again by asking Rumjhum. I went home cheerless but the dusky Jamunia, Etwari the sorceress, held the key to the puzzle.

12

Doctor Ram Kumar's story saddened me, and I felt bad about my nosiness. Excess curiosity never holds well. However, the story of his life added to my respect for him.

The Raja Sahib of the Barwe State had established the Babuani Tola. He needed men to collect malgujari from the area. So, some five-odd families were summoned from Banaras and asked to settle down. These Babu Sahibs played the roles of lathait, barahil, muharrir and tahsildar for Raja Sahib. In return, they received the income from two villages.

The same families had now increased to forty-odd families. Adjoining the Babuani Tola was the Ghansi Tola. The Ghansis were Dalits who would earn their livelihood through selling objects made from bamboo. But the new forest laws and the greed of forest guards had made bamboo such a rare article for them that their earnings had dwindled to a mere trickle. They had been reduced from artisans to landless labourers. Poverty had made them miserable. Their daughters and daughters-in-law were favourite objects for the lads and middle-aged widowers from the Babuani clan to demonstrate their virility upon.

The result of the generation-old sexual imposition was that the facial and physical features of many of the boys and girls of Ghansi Tola had taken on the aspect of people from the Babuani clan. Things had come to such a pass that if the girls from Ghansi Tola took to wearing fine clothes, they looked superior to the girls of the Babuanis. Their prettiness had become their nemesis. The Babuani lads thwarted every attempt on the part of the girls to get married, and if they somehow succeeded, God knew what tricks the louts played, but in a year or two there would be a deluge of widows and deserted wives in the Ghansi Tola. Like cows in the clutches of a butcher, these girls aged prematurely into old women, thanks to repeated abortions. Sadness dogged their steps. The larger community averted its face from the sharp questions swimming in their eyes. Doctor Ram Kumar was one such prickly issue, disowned both by the Babuanis and the Ghansi Tola. He led a monotonous, crushing life with his mother and sisters in a rented house in Kanari.

Since his childhood, the doctor had seen women being used as spittoons. It had a bizarre effect on him. If he saw anyone behaving scornfully with a siyani or insulting her, he would invariably lose his temper. When he had been young, he was ready to get into a fight at the drop of a hat, but eventually he learnt to control himself. He personally had a lot of respect for the siyanis. Be it Ramrati or Budhani, everyone was respectable to him. That's why all the sick and suffering siyanis from the paat went to him for their treatments. They knew he would keep their secrets under wraps. Their unwavering faith in him had curbed the birth of illegitimate children on the paat. Whenever he saw the angry boys of the Kanari Navayuvak Samgha, he was secretly delighted. Little by little, he channelized his fury.

The common grievance in everyone's family—be it Madan, Shyam, James or Philip—was that a mother or a sister or an aunt or a sister-in-law had been violated by the Babuanis. Naturally, they did not hesitate for a moment when it came to ganging up against the Babuani and the Gonu clans. Confrontations were routine affairs for them. Their grit had enabled them to survive in Koelbigha. It is said that when the Naxalite Jungle Party set out at night after the climb down the hills and forests north of the Koel, it stopped only at the bamboo groves, by the houses of Madan, Shyam and Philip at Jamun Toli, next to the woods. The boys brought meals for the Jungle Party. Nobody had checked out the veracity of the report, but the rumour had dampened the spirits of the Babuanis.

When Rumjhum came to James's house by the bazaar taand early Thursday morning, the boy was still asleep. But he got up on his arrival, and soon, all of them were sitting by a pond in Jamuni Tola, trying to find a solution to their problems. As expected, the moment they heard the names Gonu and Babuani, they agreed to join forces. But the memorandum they were drafting grew a little extensive. The matters did not stop at the investigation into the murder of Lalchan's uncle. They insisted on launching an inquiry into the issue of the Babuanis' land, which had grown bigger than the ceiling limits, as well as the land issues of the Gonu clan. Portions had been encroached upon by the Chote Sahib of Tori-Kamti and the Upadhyay family, too. It had all been mentioned in the letter.

The most vital issue was the mining—legal and illegal—on the paat. The writers wanted to examine the terms of lease of the mining companies and complained about the administrative negligence of the last thirty years. The very first clause in the lease agreement, of the mining companies' duty to fill the cavities left after excavation, was being impudently flouted. The companies did not spend a single penny of their profits on the development of the people on the paat. There were no facilities for drinking water, or hospitals, or measures to check the spread of malaria and diarrhoea. The local boys were never considered for any kind of employment higher than common wage labourers, despite their Intermediate and BA degrees.

The memorandum kept growing, but at least it now addressed everyone's concerns. A group consisting of Lalchan Da, Rumjhum and James Lakra visited all the villages on the paat. The impact was much higher than they had anticipated. Work was stopped not only in the Koelbigha Block mines, but also in the adjoining areas. A gigantic crowd came to the district headquarters. When the rally moved from Birsa Maidan, the whole city was covered in green flags. The city had never witnessed such a large procession of villagers, tribal folk and labourers. Budhani Di and Etwari were at the forefront, carrying a banner of the Samgharsh Samiti. I had not been allowed to join them. James, on a motorcycle, had the duty of keeping an eye on everything. It was made clear to the collector once they handed over the memorandum that they wouldn't tolerate a sham enquiry. Work at the mines, blocks and circles would remain at a standstill until a genuine investigation took place.

The bureaucrats and press correspondents were used to talking to intellectuals and businessmen, and political leaders who moved about in luxurious cars. They did not take this rustic crowd, the Asur-Kol boys, seriously. But when production had been at a standstill for three days, they grew restless. When, on the seventh day, a peaceful crowd of women stopped the advance of the heavy vehicles of the armed forces near Patharpaat, frowns appeared on the foreheads of the administration for the first time.

However, Doctor Ram Kumar, Lalchan, Rumjhum and James Lakra had failed to grasp a vital fact. Investigation into the murder of Lalchan Da's uncle and the issue of land encroachment and stopping work in the block and circle offices was one thing, but by halting production in thirty to forty mines on the paat, they had challenged the new gods openly. The current incarnations were the heaven-cruising occupants of the Global Village. They displayed exceptional solidarity. The seven-day ceasing of work in the mines and the return of the armed forces had seriously upset these lords.

13

The outcome of their anxiety was predictable. The Celestial God relayed his message to all spheres personally. His powerful devotees in this small settlement stirred into action. Of them, the First Devotee was Sri Kishan Kanhaiya Pandey, manager of the Shindalco company.

Pandey Baba had been the topper of the batch of '71 at his mining college. After passing out, he did not have to sit idle for a single day. It is a lucky fellow who can find employment in a firm in his native place. He was also fortunate enough to get a gentle, comely wife and beget a Barbie doll-like daughter. But the wife left him prematurely, passing away after a conjugal life of fifteen years. Pandeyji married his daughter off at a tender age. The groom, working in Elysium-like New York, was a high-caste Brahmin youth. The idea behind the early wedlock was that the daughter would spend her days in bliss there, and also pursue her studies. Having fulfilled all his familial responsibilities, Pandeyji began leading a single life again at the age of fifty.

True to his name, Kishan Kanhaiya Pandey had been voyeuristic since childhood, but the streak had remained largely dormant, occasionally surfacing during his visits to Delhi, Mumbai or Thailand. But now, he felt unfettered. The nearly empty Bhelwapaat Colony of Shindalco gave him free reins. Bachelor probationary officers preferred to stay together in the guest house. The quarters of the clerical staff were some distance from the bungalows of the senior officers. For him, the most delightful thing was that girls were aplenty in the rural settlements adjacent to the colony. The elders in the settlements believed that the number of girls in their community was more than desirable; moreover, girls are like rivers, each finding her course on her own. Pandey Baba exploited their matriarchal set-up to his benefit. Silver coins spin faster on the slippery track of poverty. A residential training centre for the nuns of a religious institution in Bhelwapaat seemed to be lucre added to beauty in his eyes.

Pandeyji's voyeurism did not concur with the philosopher Vatsyayan on many counts. He did not agree with the *Kama Sutra*'s limited classification of women into Padmini, Chitrini or Hastini. His decades' worth of experience in different lands had extended his range. No female was anathema to him—be she bashful or middle-aged or elderly or fair or black. There had been a rush of white Russian women after the disintegration of the USSR; he carried their mobile numbers in his diary. Only a two-hour flight from Delhi and a four-hour road journey from the state capital: everything was within reach because the World Village was now truly global.

Slim and trim, and with a well-preserved physique, Pandeyji was still quite energetic, a strict disciplinarian. He would enter his chamber at the stroke of nine-thirty in the morning and return after a visit to the field post-lunch, leaving the office on the dot at six-thirty every evening. After that, he spent his time as he desired, until midnight. There were facilities for a variety for games at the guest house—billiards, tennis, badminton— whatever you wanted.

Behind the bungalow was a swimming pool, where he and his guests would frolic with the beauties. A tanker-load of water was brought every morning for this small but enticing pool. Pandeyji maintained that in this desolate forested paat, where no manager had ever cared to stay for more than fifteen months, he had spent fifteen years in the service of the nation, and therefore, he could also claim a little bit of service from the nation in return. His hospitality was even-handed. Whether it was an officer from the district office or a VVIP from the national capital, he welcomed everyone with an open heart. Years of experience had taught him that the local visitors went gaga over white women, while the VVIPs from the outside liked the local, ethnic-looking girls. Pandey Baba had transformed this isolated wooded zone into an oasis.

Vehicles sporting yellow beacons graced the gates of the guest house every evening.

It was not that Pandey Baba was not religiously inclined. He was a Brahmin, and it ran in his blood. Whenever he noticed a virgin, he would immerse himself in tantric meditation with her. Sometimes, the trance continued all night. It was said that he had gained hypnotic powers through these meditation sessions. Whoever came in contact with him became his avowed disciple forever.

As a matter of fact, the Sakhuapaat unit of Shindalco had been turning a profit for the last fifteen years. Naturally, the management had full faith in the abilities of their senior manager. But this time, things had stretched a bit too far. Doubts were being expressed about whether Pandey was getting old and toothless.

Manager Kishan Kanhaiya Pandey had encountered several bandhs and picketing by dozens of political parties during his long term, and had tackled them all successfully. He could read, at a glance, the minds of the leaders when they arrived with their lengthy petitions. This was the secret to his success. He made clandestine arrangements to satisfy everyone's needs, keeping in mind the concerned person's stature. Almost all the parties received monthly payments from him. Some were given petty contracts and challans were forged for others, all done to make the illegally extracted ore legitimate. But now, for the first time in his life, he felt that this bloody quartet of Ram Kumar,

Lalchan, Rumjhum and James were not submitting to his chicanery, unlike all the others.

Then someone told Pandey Sahib that James's sister, Saloni Lakra, was an assistant in the main branch of the company. Enlightenment dawned upon him. He recalled the bashful Saloni from Kanari. She had grown up under his care. Now the cards were in his hand. The senior management had to be shown that Pandey could never become irrelevant.

Saloni Lakra was transferred to the Sakhuapaat office overnight. She was summoned to a confidential meeting in Pandeyji's chamber the moment she joined the branch. There were several strange faces present, along with the local leaders of a number of political parties, as well as Ansari, the contractor, and Ramrati. Saloni's role was scripted. The job was indispensable for her to feed the family and it was crucial to follow the boss's orders to retain it. The same evening, a jeep screeched to a halt outside Kanari, and Ramrati and Saloni got down.

James flew into a rage at first when Saloni tried to persuade him to agree. He refused to give in. Finally, Ramrati pulled an old video cassette out of her bag. Its contents stunned Saloni and James. It was a cassette from the days of Pandeyji's tutelage of Saloni, of the tantra meditation sessions. Ramrati informed them coolly that Pandey Baba had many such cassettes in his possession.

The brother and sister broke into sobs, avoiding each

other's eyes. Ramrati's crooked smile proved that Pandey Baba's antidote had been effective after all.

Meanwhile, the district collector, Sinha Sahib, received an angry phone call from the capital in the early hours of the morning. The conversation was so harsh that he began quaking in his shoes. It was only after running from pillar to post that he had extricated himself from the dry grind of the Secretariat. Even after his promotion to the IAS, he had been shuttled from one department to the other, now a Director in this department, now the Special Secretary in that. The direct IAS recruits did not let him join their ranks and Sinha Sahib himself never condescended to becoming pally with the juniors of the Provincial Civil Service to which he had earlier belonged. His retirement was barely two years away. His daughters had to be married off and his son also had to be settled. He had bought a plot in the capital long ago, and now he wanted to build a house there. If he remained stuck in the Finance Department as Director or Special Secretary of Planning, he would never be able to do any of this. His back ached when he remembered the prostrations he had had to make at many doors and thresholds.

He did not want his years of slogging to be fruitless simply because the Kols, Kirats and tribal Asurs were obstinate. He trusted in the saying that it was impossible to convince a Kol and digest the root oal. They only understood the language of kicks in the back; they could not be won over with reasonable arguments.

It was by Pandeyji's grace that the Kanari Navayuwak Samgha withdrew their agitation. What James and Philip, and Madan and Shyam received was of another order, but the police raided the paat the very night the demands were dropped and arrested dozens of Asurs like Doctor Ram Kumar, Lalchan, Ramchan, Rumjhum, Soma, Bhikha, Gandoor and the still convalescing Balchan.

The next morning, work resumed in all the mines except Sakhuapaat. The workers of the Sakhuapaat Shindalco Mines staged a picket in the middle of the road, led by Budhani Di. There was no point starting work; neither the trucks from below nor those carrying bauxite to the foothills were allowed to move. That night, Budhani Di was also taken into custody.

14

Lalchan, Rumjhum and their colleagues spent only a few days in jail. Shivdas Baba of Koel Ashram bailed them out. This Baba had been running a monastery and a school in Koelbigha for years. He had also initiated an amulet-wearing and purification mission. But he had not been able to make inroads into the Asuri village yet. His move took Lalchan and Rumjhum by surprise.

In fact, until this time, the Asur community and the paat had not been a part of Baba's plan. Vidhayakji wanted to arrange a ceremonious yajna and homage on the paat to facilitate repeated visits by the Baba. But now, could there be a better way to connect with the Asur community? Baba came to the town himself. It has been rightly said that you laugh and the world laughs with you, suffer and you suffer alone. Even your shadow deserts you at such a time. But Baba maintained that only a true human being could understand the misery of another. Baba's charismatic personality, his ochre clothes, his radiant forehead and silver tongue won everybody over.

People believed that Shivdas Baba had appeared in the Shiv temple on the bank of the Koel in Kanari village some seven-odd years ago. It was said that he had sat down in meditation in the Koeleshwar temple. His disciples told everyone that Baba was the reincarnation of Baba Jatreshwar Nath. Like him, Baba was also the Enlightened One.

Once, when he was taking a bath in his village pond, a light flashed from heaven and suffused him. He was a university top ranker, a really talented boy. His parents had extremely high hopes for him. He could easily compete in the IAS exams, but his life changed all of a sudden. The Koel river and a Shiv temple haunted him in his dreams. After all, why should a person from around Ayodhya suddenly come to stay in this temple? How did he recall the river, the temple and Baba Jatreshwar Nath? It was nothing short of a miracle.

Bit by bit, Baba's amulet mission began to gather momentum. He started visiting the villages. He would arrange a fire-homa and initiate the disciples in the wearing of the amulet. The amulet-wearer did not have to take many pains; he had to merely follow a few simple rules. He had to become a vegetarian and refrain from hanriya or wine. A tulsi had to be planted in his courtyard and a peepal tree in his compound. Sorcery, witchcraft, shamans, ghosts, ghouls, witches—he had to shun all these. The siyanis had to touch their husbands' feet reverently, both when they woke up and when they went to bed. Every Thursday, the amulet-wearers had to assemble in the akhra to sing hymns. They could not even drink water offered by someone outside the amulet community. Hygiene had to be maintained diligently and the disciples had to avoid black cloth, black objects, black cattle or hens or pigs. For them, the black creatures were not actually animals but ghouls in disguise. The devotees had to keep them at bay at any cost.They could not afford to be lax. Disrespect to the amulet put a curse on the bearer. Baba had under his control a spirit that ruined any disciples who offended the amulet. Or that was what Baba's followers said. They had dozens of such tales. Nothing else was required. The man being initiated had to offer some money to Baba as well. But the offering had to be small. Baba never accepted more than a hundred rupees from one disciple.

The news of his healing power, his energy and his blessing spread so fast that the Thursday congregation in the ashram became as huge as a fair. People arrived, loaded on vehicles and carts, not only from the Koelbigha block but also from other blocks and districts.

The worst sufferers were the black creatures. No amulet-wearing disciple ever agreed to have anything to do with black cattle, hens or pigs. They were not willing to tolerate the mute creatures for a single day. There was such an influx of black animals in the haat that their prices hit rock bottom. The traders were quick to seize upon this opportunity. They purchased these animals at throwaway prices, pretending they were doing a good turn to their masters.

When truck after truck started leaving the haat with the cattle, the administration was roused from its deep slumber. At first, drums were beaten and announcements were made in the haats, hitting out against the superstition. When things did not improve, the administration issued orders that no peasant could sell more than one animal at a time in the haat. But Baba's disciples were more afraid of the ghouls than they were of the administration. They were not willing to accept that the cattle were not only animals, but also their capital, and the passbook of their household bank. During illness and disease, marriages and engagements, in short, on all occasions, they were of much use. However, Shivdas Baba's miracle emptied the household deposits in a single stroke and the twist was that the villagers were not even remotely aware of it.

The cattle traders did not reap much profit either. The reality was that Baba's men had already extracted the best possible price of the cattle from them. The profit had exceeded the Baba's expectations. In fact, right after the black creature bubble burst, the grand opening of Baba's ashram and school took place.

Baba was very particular about the education of girls. He used to say that boys could go anywhere for studies, but girls were constrained and occupied by household work.

This led to half of the country staying illiterate. This was, to him, the biggest impediment to the country's enjoying the status of a world guru. To overcome this, he built an imposing high school with a boarding facility for girls on the gair-majurwa or community land next to the ashram. Babaji personally oversaw the building—a well-planned hostel, mess, library, fields for games and a laboratory—even though an official committee comprising the town intelligentsia was formed for the purpose.

To leave no stone unturned in his effort to build the character of the girls, Baba took special care to employ only female staff and teachers for his venture. A small entrance was left open between Baba's ashram and the girls' hostel, so that they might receive the holy effects of his evening prayers, the worship ceremony and the fire-homa and thus imbibe strong moral values. Babaji laid special emphasis on this. He was a staunch supporter of ancient Indian values as well as of modern science and education.

Baba believed that the Macaulay education system was a worm burrowing into the foundations of a deeply religious country like India. A series of ashram schools were built to offset the ill-effects of this edict. Schools were started in other districts too, based on the growing demands of his disciples. Baba did not believe in discrimination between boys and girls, so an ashram-cum-guest house was constructed on the campus of each of the schools. Occasionally, Baba would consecrate the guest houses with his visits. If the girls' schools were preferred for his nightly stops, it could in no way be considered a weakness but simply the victory of faith and veneration. However, the detractors had filthy minds and often came up with objectionable accusations. Why should one encourage such sinful fellows? The famous poet, Tulsi Baba, wrote centuries ago, 'One perceives his God as he is himself.'

Now and then, a couple of nasty lady teachers would charge Baba—in front of the intelligentsia committee—with accusations of indulging in immoral activities, but there was never any ready proof. The members considered it sacrilege to even imagine such things about their God-like Baba. They rejected the accusations as the concoctions of wicked women. It was improper even to let the shadow of these immoral women touch the righteous girls in the schools. Naturally, they were kicked out post-haste. It was by God's grace that a couple of female teachers with divine thoughts came forward and spent their weekdays providing personalized service to Baba. Baba's blessings gratified such devoted lady disciples and in the blink of an eye, their houses transformed from humble mud constructions to gilded edifices with golden spires and silver doors from which sweet jingling emanated.

There was an interesting episode from the early days of Baba's career, when a stupid Officer-in-Charge discovered the naked corpse of a twelve- or thirteen-year-old girl in the bushes by the river next to the ashram. A garland of lemon and chillies around her neck, hibiscus blossoms in her hair, and sindoor marks on the torso and limbs... it was obvious that the girl had been the victim of some occult ritual. The silly Officer-in-Charge arrested Baba, but he had not reckoned with the man's clout. When he was taken to the lock-up, the tribal people and the Sadaans from the neighbouring villages descended on the roads and blocked them by felling large trees growing on the sides. The collector and the SP started receiving frantic telephone calls from their superiors. The officers left for the Koelbigha Block even before the wireless message reached them from the police thana. Eventually, the imprudent Officer-in-Charge had to beg forgiveness from Baba by touching his feet and releasing him; only then was the matter sorted out.

Impressed by his purification mission, his aura of knowledge, moral fibre and value-imbibing schools, a culture-policing, morality-protectorate political party enrolled Baba as an honoured member. And when Babaji played a vital role in the party's Janmbhoomi Movement, sending thousands of his disciples to the 'birth land', his stature grew considerably. He became part of this moral-righteous party's think tank.

Babaji also played an important role in the distribution of party tickets to candidates in the next elections. A sizeable number of his disciples got tickets. One of them was elected to the Lok Sabha, three to the Vidhan Sabha.

Belief in Babaji's stature grew so weighty that the earth started doddering. It was a mere coincidence that the party formed governments in both the centre and the state.

Now, Goddess Laxmi, and Lords Kuber, Varuna and Indra became permanent residents in the ashram. A retired but worldly-wise IAS officer got an NGO registered without being prompted by Baba. Another retired IAS officer put together a team of professionals like civil engineers, agriculture scientists, veterinary doctors and horticulture experts. The rest of the work was done by their junior officers. Money started pouring in. Where to store it? How to spend it? This posed a big problem.

Naturally, when such an exalted Baba came personally to bail out Lalchan, Rumjhum and his ilk, astonishment was quite a normal reaction.

15

Lalchan Da was overwhelmed by Shivdas Baba. Now, the desi cabin at Budhani Di's echoed with Babaji's legends. *Babaji is so powerful, Babaji is so great. Babaji said this, Babaji said that.* All day long, nothing but Baba's name. Lalchan Da was wholly taken in.

With one phone call from Babaji, Section 144 was imposed on the paddy field in Mahua Toli. The enquiry into the murder of Lalchan Da's uncle was handed over to the crime branch and the matter of the illegal settlement of government land and occupation of land beyond ceiling limits by Gonu Singh was handed to a magistrate. The magistrate actually came down to the circle office to examine the land records and assured them he would visit again. Babaji's wish was their command. Everyone took these matters seriously.

At the ashram, Babaji organized a meeting of the mine owners and managers. A small hitch remained, related to the filling of the abandoned open mines. Many of the managers argued that a geological survey had to be conducted to find out whether further bauxite deposits existed there or not. The survey had somehow been put off for years, and as a result, the ditches had not been levelled.

But Lalchan and Rumjhum were clear on this point. It was not a matter of a year or two. They had never seen any filling work, not in all the years they had grown up there, no matter whether the mines belonged to a powerful stakeholder like Shindalco or less significant ones like Poddar and Rungta. The companies were concerned only with the production of bauxite. After mining, they found the cost of filling the mines exorbitant, in spite of their profit growing into millions and billions. These fellows would not spend a single paisa on the paat. The fact of the matter was that they did not consider the paat people human beings. Mosquitoes breeding in the rainwater collected in these mines had made their lives hell. Forget the old people, more than four dozen young boys had died of cerebral malaria already. But had the miners ever sympathized with the community? They were only concerned with their profits.

Babaji raised a hand to interrupt the harangue. It was decided that the ditches would have to be filled. Boys from the Asur community would have to be given positions in the mining offices. Instructions to undertake measures like the provision of potable water and the building of a small hospital were also unwillingly accepted by the companies.

After this, Lalchan Da became a staunch follower of

Babaji. Rumjhum kept fuming, but Lalchan Da was so witlessly blind in his devotion that he was not open to reason. Kavita and Namita were taken out of my school and admitted in the boarding school at Koeleshwar Ashram. Lalchan immersed himself in the task of visiting different localities, making preparations for the fire-homa that would be performed by Babaji. A surge of amulet-wearers arose on the paat as well.

Rumjhum continued seething alone at Budhani Di's tea stall. He did not even feel like talking to me. Doctor Sahib laughed at Lalchan's conversion. He tried to convince Rumjhum that the ardour was new, and it would take some time to vanish. 'Let time pass', he said. Lalchan would come to his senses.

But I could sense the reasons for Rumjhum's annoyance with me. Gandoor must have complained. In recent months, Etwari had gone overboard. She had become addicted to me. On the other hand, the amethyst tint had begun to fade from my heart. I felt we now shared only a carnal relationship, nothing else. There was no novelty to it any more. Now Jamunia did not remind me of the moonlight, gulainchi or the melody or the Phuljhar spring. The overbearing shadow of the flesh had eclipsed everything else. Now there was only a body, one that was getting staler by the day.

It was hard for me to watch this dusky blossom wither away. I wanted to preserve the moonlight, the fragrance of the gulainchi, the heady romance of the Asuri songs and the chime of the Phuljhar spring. When I started sleeping with the door of my room bolted on the inside, she would tickle the soles of my feet with a kaner twig to wake me up. When I closed the window the next night, she used a steel wire to slide down the bolt of the door. I was out of my depth. How could I stop the amethyst fading from my heart?

Sure, Gandoor's complaint was justified; he had a right to complain. However, the fault was not entirely mine. It was that of the night too, and the moon that had shared the hanriya, the brazen way it had consorted with Gandoor on the grass, and the gulainchi who had left me alone with Jamunia on that solitary night. But who would have believed me? And why, after all?

16

Several months had passed since the agreement had been inked, but there were no visible signs of implementation. The bigger companies like Shindalco had filled two or three abandoned quarries by the road as window-dressing. Some of the important Asur youths like Rumjhum, Soma and Bhikha were given jobs in the office, but they did not seem very happy. They were routinely humiliated in the name of training. The employers did not care for Rumjhum's knowledge of history, or his Honours degree in Sanskrit. His aim was to work as a mate with the labourers in the field, but he was handed account books which he absolutely hated. Whenever he made a mistake, everyone made fun of him, including the peon from the Poddar Mining office, Dubey. This hurt Rumjhum terribly.

The tanker carrying water to Pandeyji's bungalow at Bhelwapaat now made an additional trip. During the day, it would stay parked in the Sakhuapaat bazaar. Its water brought some relief to the siyanis in the areas nearby. But there was still no project to lift water from a spring, waterfall or stream with the help of an electric pump. The management did not bother about its promises of a hospital either.

After a few days, James Lakra and his friends, who had been hiding their faces all this time, started zooming around on sparkling new motorbikes. One had become a petty contractor, another had been gifted a second-hand truck. This was the award for the quislings. No boy from the paat talked to them now. Many scuffles were barely avoided at Budhani's tea stall. The tension between Kanari and the paat was so high that Doctor Sahib had to shift his residence to Sakhuapaat, where he now lived with his mother and sister.

There were no signs of the earlier unity or peace on the paat. Pointless fights took place between the amulet-wearers and the other folks. Lalchan had still not outgrown his infatuation with Babaji. Finally, Ram Kumar took stringent measures. No one but he really knew about Baba's tricks and hypocrisy. Doctor Sahib vented all his frustration to me in one breath one day.

He had been escorted from his Kanari residence to the ashram in secret many nights. So many times he had saved the lives of the young girls lying in Baba's room by administering glucose and water intravenously, so many times, that he had lost count. Whenever his eyes fell on the rascal Baba, he felt like spitting in his face. The swine was a pervert in need of mental treatment. Baba lost control whenever he came across a woman alone, no matter how old. He turned into a vicious animal after taking narcotics like cannabis and bhang. His perversions had acquired psychopathic dimensions since the boarding schools had been established. He demanded young girls every night to massage his legs. It had been going on for years. Who on the paat in the coal-bearing region was not aware of it? But nobody dared protest. Everyone was afraid of his reach. Criminals sporting long beards and lost in the stupor of narcotics were a common sight, always lounging in the ashram. It was a terror tactic. People were afraid of his authority over the police and the administration.

Doctor Sahib had two nagging issues he wanted to stand up for. One was the masquerade concerning the black creatures. The cattle of the poor Asurs should not have been sold at throwaway rates in the haat. When Lalchan demurred, Doctor Sahib sent a couple of boys to catch hold of a small-time trader from Sakhuapaat. The fellow was put in a room and thrashed with shoes. He squealed quickly about how much he and the other traders had had to pay to the ashram for every animal they bought. Only then did Lalchan see the light and his craze for Baba abated a little.

The other issue was that there was no protein in the staple diet of the paat Asurs. In the name of pulses, they would be given a tiny amount of urad along with sarguja; it was dried in dollops in the sun, along with gourds or khira. When guests arrived, the dollops were cooked in gravy and served with boiled rice as bhaat-jhor. Usually, the Asurs filled their bellies with corn or boiled rice. The only source of protein was the mutton bought from the haats that were held every three or four days, or fish caught from some spring. If they stopped eating this, the growth of the children would be stunted and the youth would become emaciated. It was not wise to turn vegetarian. Finally, after protracted arguments from both sides, it was decided that the amulet-wearers would remove their amulet while eating non-vegetarian food and put them on again after a ritual bath.

The paddy ripened luxuriantly in the rice field at Mahua Toli, but the matter of ownership had still not been sorted out. There was no progress on the murder case either. 'The magistrate has received orders for transfer. The new one has not taken charge yet.' There were one hundred and one excuses for the bureaucracy's dragging its feet.

Once again, Doctor Sahib had brought the news that the Gonu clan was trying to find ways to harvest the crops. They would reap the crops in the middle, leaving one hand of paddy intact on all sides to get around legal problems. Maybe they had been given the advice by the Officer-in-Charge, or by a lawyer. In any case, something had to be done quickly.

The matter had to be kept secret from Balchan, but would it be possible? He had just recovered from his injuries. His appetite had barely improved over the last three or four weeks. The shine and laughter had just come back into his face. Nobody wanted him to take a rash step out of anger. The family's finances had suffered badly during his medical treatment. They were not ready for trouble yet.

That night, Balchan stole out of the house silently. Nobody at home suspected anything, not even his gomkain who had been lying by his side. God knows how he managed it, but the first stack of paddy crops lay in the barnyard before the break of dawn. There was a whisper that he had taken the help of his mates from the Jungle Party. Others said he had gone with his friends after collecting ash from the cremation grounds. He had blown the ash towards Mahua Toli and the whole village had fallen into so deep a slumber that nobody even heard a creak. Whatever had happened, the family's paddy had come home.

17

Lalchan Da informed me that his niece, Lalita, had come home for the holidays after writing her exams. On the way, she had visited Kavita and Namita at their boarding school. They looked ill, so she had brought them home as well. They wouldn't tell her anything, but their aunt said they had had a fight with someone in the ashram. 'Go ask them,' she told me. 'Maybe they'll tell you.'

On Saturday night, I went to Ambatoli as usual. Rumjhum avoided me. Maybe it was the pressure of his job in the Poddar mines, or perhaps it was because of Gandoor's complaint. The job was really becoming a pain for him. I didn't want to complicate matters. Soma and Bhikha told me that he was always drunk on mahua these days. He had become an alcoholic, bunking office frequently. 'You could never tell, bloody Poddar might chuck him from his job at any time.'

Lalchan Da, Doctor Sahib, everyone was sick of Rumjhum's growing addiction. They knew why it had happened. Rumjhum had told them about every little attempt made in the office to humiliate him. He had quoted the venomous jibes of Mishraji, Vermaji, and the peon, Dubeyji. He should have nipped the problem in the bud. Now things had gotten out of hand.

Lalchan Da recalled the discussion of that day regretfully, saying that if everyone had taken the manager of Poddar mines to task right at the start, Rumjhum might have got his favourite job in the field. Things would not have come to this pass. Just the previous night, he had bruised himself badly after slipping and falling on the trail to his house in Kandapaat, and hurt his head.

Lalita came in with the tea right then. Lalchan Da had told me quite early on that although Lalita was his niece, she was more like a daughter to him. His elder brother and his wife had died of malaria in the same year, within a span of six months. Lalita, barely fourteen, had been studying in the seventh class then. She was a studious girl. After the death of her Ayo and Baba, she became an introvert, immersing herself in books. Naturally, her aunt's fondness for her grew. Lalchan and his wife took care not to hinder her studies. When she was in the tenth class and then in the eleventh, Rumjhum came home regularly to help her with her studies. She had passed with excellent marks. Now she was doing her MA, but she was still a very quiet girl.

When had she come in? When did she greet me with a johar? When did she return after serving the tea? I did not remember anything. I just kept staring at her. On the paat at least, I had never seen such a cultured, decently attired, comely girl. She was not as fair as Lalchan's family, but her wheatish complexion had a beatific glow. Taller than the average local girl and slim, she had a grandness of bearing that reminded me of someone from the pages of history. I tried to recollect who, knowing I had read a book recently about someone with such a personality. In a moment, the name of Pocahontas came back to me.

The English founded their first settlement, Jamestown, in Virginia in 1607. But the Native Americans disliked their activities. The chief of the local community, Powatan, imprisoned one of the senior English army officials, but the day he was to be killed, Princess Pocahontas saved the captain's life. She also helped the English residents of Jamestown in secret many times. She saved their lives but in return, they imprisoned her by tricking her with an invitation to their ship. She was forcibly married to an English trader, John Rolf, a widower, and taken to London. London went crazy over the royal demeanour and graceful aura of the princess. Sir Walter Raleigh came to visit her. The poet, Ben Jonson, gazed at her for hours. He was too stunned to speak in her presence. But this daughter of Nature could not endure the polluted environs of London for long. She contracted TB and passed away at the unripe age of twenty-two.

On the other hand, the English almost wiped out her

community after Powatan's death. From eight thousand, their population dwindled to a measly one thousand. They were scattered and perished over the course of time.

Why did Lalita remind me of Princess Pocahontas? Was it a signal from Destiny? Was Lalita's Asur community also going to scatter and perish? Why this apprehension? Did my left eye start twitching to warn me of the future?

Lalchan Da's Baba called him in. I took a magazine from my bag and started turning the pages. Just then, Lalita came out with Bhauji. They wanted Kavita and Namita to be admitted at the Bhaunrapaat School again. Bhauji told me that Lalita was not willing to send them to the Koeleshwar School again, even for a single day. God knows which of Baba's bearded disciples had crossed Lalita's path and had started molesting her in the name of offering blessings. There was pandemonium when she slapped him. The girls also looked sickly. They neither ate properly, nor were they their usual selves. What would their grandfather say if he found out? 'You please take them to Doctor Sahib for a medical check up,' Bhauji said to me.

When I passed through the courtyard and entered the girls' room, I almost failed to recognize them. Their faces had withered; they had lost a lot of weight. Sunken eyes. Dry lips. They looked as though they had been sick for months. My first thought was to summon Doctor Sahib.

Doctor Sahib realized the seriousness of the matter at

once. He started grumbling that even a witch keeps off at least seven neighbouring households, but this rascal Baba was a fiend. He must have summoned the girls to massage his legs at night. The girls had been petrified after such shocking assaults. 'I have already seen dozens of such cases in the ashram,' Doctor Sahib said to me. 'The bastard has gulped down all his sense of shame, disgrace and fear.'

Muttering, he collected medicine, injections and vitamins and rode in the truck with me. He talked to the girls alone. His hunch was right. Their tender hearts had been traumatized, leading to their loss of appetite and peace of mind. They saw the naked, demonic Baba everywhere. The only treatment they needed was care and understanding, and medicine to induce sleep and appetite. The nursing duties were explained to Lalita.

Standing at a distance during this conversation, I nevertheless felt that Lalita was asking Doctor Ram Kumar about me. I don't know what he told her but at least now she no longer looked wary. I could see some warmth in her eyes.

18

The girls responded well to the treatment, and recovered within a few weeks. They were readmitted to the Bhaunrapaat School. Lalita escorted the girls personally into the chamber of the headmistress and completed the admission formalities. I didn't have to lift a finger. At first, she accompanied Kavita and Namita every morning. She would send them into the classroom and sit for a while with Madam Minj. I found out that she had been her favourite student. A couple of days later, it came to light that she would conduct classes at school when she came home for holidays. This was helpful, because Rumjhum had started playing truant after three every afternoon. However, Etwari did not look happy at all. Her eyes hardened whenever they fell on Lalita.

Our frequent meetings in school broke the ice between us. Moreover, everyone doted on Lalita's honey-sweet voice. Everybody was eager to talk to her, except Etwari, whose expressions and manner showered glowing embers upon her.

Lalita was pretty cross with her uncle, Lalchan Ka. She believed that men, especially Asur men, were gullible and could be cheated easily. They had not learnt any lesson from their tragic lore. She had very high expectations of her Rumjhum Ka. She believed he was far superior to his brother, and her classmate, Sunil Asur, that there was absolutely no ground for comparison between the two. She tried to see Rumjhum several times. Once, when she went to the Poddar mines office at Sakhuapaat, the staff members began ogling her and whispering in quite a lewd manner. She felt like a new animal in the zoo. The mulish Dubey crossed all limits of decency and burst into an obscene Bhojpuri song. The rest of them were no better. Men old enough to be her father and grandfather—flabby, sagging, elderly Mishraji, Sinhaji, Verma, Sharma and Guptaji—began acting in a strange manner. One kept grinning, another started talking in whispers, and yet another suffered a non-stop bout of coughing. One of them took out his purse to flaunt currency at her. God knew what they took her for! Was she the water-maid in their houses, or Ramrati? She sat at Rumjhum Ka's table for barely three or four minutes. She felt as if her head would explode or that she would catch hold of one of the louts and beat him black and blue. The molten iron running through her veins had not turned to water yet.

Sometimes, she went to Kandapaat to talk to Rumjhum Ka, but he was never in his senses. Rumjhum Ka's gomkain held her close, crying about her husband's descent into the abyss.

Lalita often tried to rediscover her old Rumjhum Ka, who used to come every day to teach her with all seriousness, as though he were impatient to pour into her all his knowledge of the world. Each piece of information he presented to her was unique and brilliant. It opened new portals of light every moment, lending thousands of wings to her fancy. With the help of this learning, she would take off on the journey through time. She would be here only bodily, while her imagination soared into strange horizons. She would tour the cosmos, all the while sitting in Ambatoli. She could clearly see the features of all the countries and the continents. All the civilizations danced before her eyes as if in a TV serial. Every subject would become pleasurable and light, like dewdrops, and then it would be hard to believe that Rumjhum was simply instructing her, not narrating a grandmotherly fairy tale.

Each of her failures to revive the old image of Rumjhum Ka forced her to retreat further into herself. When she felt she would go berserk if she did not let someone into her thoughts, she turned to me. Perhaps our daily meetings had made her trust me. When she, as graceful as Princess Pocahontas, began to look for time to talk to me, it seemed only natural that I should develop a swagger. If I felt helpless like the poet, Ben Jonson, it was not my fault. When she sat by me, a languorous fragrance would waft in the breeze. But when she grew agitated, she would talk so animatedly that heat waves seemed to radiate from her, as if molten metals were flowing by. It was a heat so terribly intense.

One Sunday in Ambatoli, she appeared to be in an ecstatic mood, as if wishing to cast away all her frustrations through her insight into the Sing-Bonga legend. 'What's this Sing-Bonga legend? Sing-Bonga assumed the disguise of a khasra boy not only to fool the Asurs but also burnt them all to cinders in the furnace. However, it shouldn't be taken literally. The Asurs were killed in the battle by fraud. The remarkable fact is that only the men from the Asur community were duped, not the women. In the tale too, the Asur women acted wisely and put up resistance. They held the legs of the flying Sing-Bonga and made efforts to stop him. But they had to pay a heavy price, becoming witches and ghosts in the legend.

'In our times too, this amulet movement, the fire-homa, the hymns, this naked Baba—what's all this? Is not Kaka deceiving himself? We are Nature worshippers. Our Lord, All-compassionate Mahadeva, is not Langta Baba's god. Our Mahadeva is this hill, this paat, which sustains us. Our Sarna Mai suffuses not only the sakhua tree but the flora all around. We include all creatures in our gotra. We respect even the smallest insect; we simply don't have the concept of the "other". A community that has nurtured such a beautiful concept, what need does it have to seek the shelter of Langta Baba or any other fellow? But no, whenever a new chap arrives, he tricks and converts us. Still, we have the gall to claim we are Asurs with breasts of steel and arms of arkanthe. When we mention our ancestors, we deify them and raise them to lofty heights, right up to the top of the tree, talking of iron smelting and steel coursing through their veins. But when we fall, we realize that in reality even water does not run in our bodies.

'What is the use of this movement? First, we had to serve jail sentences. Then there was this agreement. Where are the clauses now? Where are the murderers of my uncle? Have we got back our paddy field? Are the abandoned mines being plugged? Shindalco has given up even the charade of filling them. Only a couple have been filled. Is there any sign of the hospitals that were promised? Is the woe of cerebral malaria past? Even today, thugs and contractors are collecting the thumb impressions of the Asurs and Oraons on blank paper to carry on their illegal mining. The exodus of our girls to Delhi and Kolkata, to the houses of mates and munshis, is on the rise, rather than declining. What was the point of going to prison or putting on the amulet?

'Master Sahib, you claim to be a close friend of Kaka's. Go ask him. Will he do something or do we have to take up cudgels?'

~

In the desi cabin, Lalchan Da did not say a word. Rumjhum lay on the bench in a stupor. It was hard to say whether Soma and Bhikha were in their senses or not. Lalchan Da had his head bowed the whole time. Tea was served and sipped with lowered eyes. Finally, when the silence became unbearable, I broke it, and Lalchan Da began to speak in a small voice, like a gambler who has lost every possession, as if the agony were beyond endurance.

'I reminded Shivdas Baba many times that there has been no follow up on the agreement. The mine owners are sitting idle. They levelled a mine or two just to put on a show. The work has stopped. The hospital and drinking water are nowhere in sight. They have employed a few of us, but the men and their jobs are a total mismatch. They did it on purpose so that they could kick us out whenever they liked. But the rascal Baba simply nods or begins to talk of another fire-homa on the paat or of some land deal to start a school at Ambatoli Neem Taand.'

'We have been real suckers,' Soma continued.

'Let bygones be bygones. There's no use beating about the bush. We will act now on our individual strength. Paat Devta will support us. All the Asur–Oraon–Sadaan villages will have to be united in this.' Lalchan Da's optimism had not deserted him yet.

As though on cue, we were called to Doctor Sahib's clinic. A moustachioed, obese guy with the look of a sneaky politician, no older than Doctor Sahib, was sprawled in the chair. He had extremely foul breath. The betel juice had trickled from his mouth in print-like patterns on his kurta. He was exactly like the fellow described in the film song: *Sanwari suratiya, honth laal laal*—a dark visage with red, smeared lips. On the whole, he was a flaccid clown. Doctor Sahib introduced us. 'This is Guptaji. He was my classmate in college. He has joined politics and works for Shivdas Baba. He'll explain everything.'

'Hey! Don't mention the word "work". If an important person like me has to wield a hoe, what would a Kol idiot do? We shove our hands down the throats of these mine owners to snatch whatever we want! Baba tells us to extract two rupees, we take four. What Baba demands goes to Baba, and the rest is mine. Thirty-eight to forty thousand, the monthly payoff is fixed for each mine. Fixed! Do you follow?'

We listened with our mouths open. It was stunning. Since we were silent, he continued. 'Hey! Doctor! What a bunch of nincompoops you have brought in! Is my standard so low that I have to talk to such rustic dolts? I don't encourage such people. However, I am ready to do anything for your sake....'

It was intolerable. Yet another curtain had risen. We were all in the same boat, utterly crushed. Our lips were grimly pursed. With lowered heads, we returned to the shelter of Budhani Di's desi cabin.

Just then, Rumjhum stirred and stood up. He smiled at us and then broke into a laugh. We were afraid he had gone off his rocker. He climbed up onto the bench and began singing a song. It was a melancholic number, casting a net of sadness over us. The lyrics quivered in the breeze:

How shall we spend the rest of our days
It is pointless
Our night
Swears to us it will be a sinister, gloomy night
Not a single star glimmers on the horizon
Sad gusts
Lament somewhere far off
On our heels
Treads our Nemesis
A wounded deer
Hearing the running steps of his hunter pursuing him
Readies itself
For Absolute Death.

We shivered, aghast. The bleak future loomed before us. I realized that the song I had just heard came from the book about the Native Americans. It was a song that had been sung in 1686 by a famous chief, Seattle. I felt it presaged our present and future.

19

'You smell of a woman, teacher'.

It was Lalita. We were sitting by a small spring on the wooded incline near Ambatoli. Like Columbus, we had stumbled upon a unique, lovely isle lost amid the swift currents of time, much like this mountain brook. We had christened it 'companionship'. We thought and spoke like twins now. Lalita would often speak out the thought rising in my head. When I told her about the coincidence, we would break into hysterical peals of laughter. All our differences were swept away in the swift surge of innocent hilarity.

But how could I reply to such an odd question? No sooner had Lalita started coming to the school than Etwari's behaviour had transformed. The eyes that used to shower burning embers had fallen vacant now. Her female instinct had anticipated my friendship with Lalita much before I had. She tried to avoid me, but the children and Gandoor still came to my room to do their homework or to watch TV. Only Etwari had stopped coming and talking to me. Gandoor seemed happy. I was also relieved.

How did Lalita sniff a woman's scent on my body? I could not figure it out. I simply smiled.

'Look here! The scent simultaneously pulls and repulses us women. What's the mystery? Are you in a live-in relationship?'

The words 'live-in relationship' sounded awkward in this secluded, wooded spot. However, Lalita told me that the practice was new only to modern society. It had been an accepted part of life in tribal communities since ancient times. If there was some issue in a marriage, the boy and girl could live together. However, it was crucial to perform the marriage rites before their own son was married off. The parents got married first, followed by the wedding of the son or daughter, sometimes under the same marriage canopy. If they were living together due to financial problems, the betrothal was performed as soon as they could collect enough money. The live-in fad had percolated from them into modern society.

But Lalita's query still dangled in the air: whose scent is this; what riddle is this?

I protested strongly but she was not ready to listen.

She was shaking her head when Ben Jonson's spirit alighted softly in me. I gazed at her, oblivious to everything else. Words faded and sounds disappeared. Time ceased to flow. Space and time became meaningless. My eyes quenched their thirst, consuming her features. I saw a dusky rose swinging on a branch. The dainty rose was now captive in my fist; I wanted to carry it to my lips. And then it was not a rose but a green hill in whose woods I was roaming. The moon dismounted and perched atop the mahua branch. With the moon's every movement, the mahua blossoms trickled down…drip-drop…drip-drop.

The cosmos acquired worth from the dusky rose, and from the slender lunar droplet poised on the mahua bough. Without Lalita, the world was meaningless. The amber of the sun, the coolness of the moonbeams, the gush of the streams, earth's quaintness, the crimson of the buds, the jade of the leaves—all inherited sense and significance when they mingled with her. If she were not present, the universe wasn't either.

Just then, someone clapped and my reverie broke. She guffawed at my blush. 'We are going to be fast friends. Come on! This very day we will announce each other our sahiya.' Sahiya, or becoming friends through a formal declaration, was a small ritual.

Lalchan Da chuckled when he heard. 'So far I have only heard of the boy-boy sahiya or a girl-girl sahiya. Lalita is initiating a new tradition, a new custom. That's good. Lalita has selected a buddy like herself, a bookworm. A sky-gazer. A fine thing this is.'

He looked happy. Every member in the house was pleased, except Baba. Bhauji explained to me that the ritual entailed some expenses. Sahiya was a formal affair and gifts or souvenirs had to be exchanged. 'You won't get things to Lalita's liking in the haat-bazaar here,' she told me. 'Go visit the town. The ceremony will be performed this very Sunday.'

It was a brief affair. I gifted her cloth for a salwar suit, and a pen set. Lalita had bought a nice, readymade shirt for me. We exchanged gulainchi flowers. Now we could not call each other by our names but only by the term phool, for flower.

Lalchan Da had a goat slaughtered. All the young boys and girls of the community enjoyed a hearty meal and then skipped to the beat of the maandar all night. They would often pull me in but I failed to find the rhythm, dancing ineptly. Finally, I sat down by Lalchan Da.

What was this Jhoomar dance? Moving in a semi-circle, bowing, advancing, then throwing the head back, retreating. Like a breeze billowing through the green paddy crops and sending them swishing, back and forth. Like the bamboo grove swaying, supple, sportive, joining the wind. Like waves in the rivers, rising and falling sensuously. Like swarms of birds in the sky, returning to their nests. Nature herself in her primeval form, merged with the divine swing of the cosmos.

The moon set. The night, like a blanket soaked in dew, grew heavy. Everyone was swaying. But a cuckoo call kept resonating in my ears: 'Hey, phoool!'

20

The spirit in the Thursday bazaar at Sakhuapaat seemed rather low. The usual smiles were absent. Men whispered in clusters, presenting a sinister sight. Things became clear when Lalchan Da stepped into the desi cabin. 'The Forest Department has served notice to thirty-seven villages to vacate. Some new-fangled project of saving wolves. They are calling it "abhayaranya", which means sanctuary. If the word itself is so difficult to pronounce, you can imagine how complex the real thing is. Twenty-two of the villages are of the Asurs; the rest belong to Oraons, Kherwars and Sadaans.'

A hush fell.

'They'll kill human beings to save the wolf?'

'Is it a real project or a plan to kill us?'

'Is there no end to our troubles?'

'When troubles come, brother, they never come alone.'

Beads of perspiration broke out on every forehead. Everyone fell silent, bowing their heads to brood over this new crisis. Just then Rumjhum, still high, opened his eyes. He stood up to repeat over and over the same lines of a song, as if the needle of a gramophone had got stuck on the record:

The pounding of the hunters' boots
Can be heard distinctly
You cannot be saved
Wounded deer
You cannot be saved.

Defeat crept over every face. Lalchan Da pulled Rumjhum down. Lemon tea was brought to diminish his drunkenness. It was decided that a meeting would be held at Ambatoli the next day. All the baiga-pujars, pahans and the boys who knew how to read and write would attend. Information would be sent to the affected villages. This time, they had to fight their own battle.

In the middle of these arguments in Doctor Sahib's clinic, before the men left for Sakhuapaat, a message came from Shivdas Baba, brought by one of his disciples. The disciple had arrived in a truck. He wanted the centre's plan for the wolf sanctuary to be opposed at any cost. Baba would join the resistance.

We were surprised. The people of the paat and Lalchan Da hardly ever went to Baba's ashram these days. They had all taken their children out of his school, one by one. No fire-homa ceremony had been performed there for months. People had almost forgotten about his plans to start a school in Ambatoli. A number had taken off their amulets too.

'What has bitten this rascal Baba now? Why this sudden concern and sympathy?' There were plenty of doubts. The task of finding answers was delegated to Doctor Sahib.

Doctor Sahib returned with the inside story that the Forest Department had sent a report years ago, stating that earlier, the population of wolves in a 64-square-kilometre area used to be 788, but had fallen to 176. Thirty-three pages of the report had been devoted exclusively to the various unique sub-species of the wolves, the conclusion being that they had to be protected and conserved. The Forest Department had always considered the Asurs and other tribals encroachers on its land. It was not ready to pay heed to the fact that people had been living in the forest villages for hundreds of years, and that the Forest Department was the real encroacher. Like the animals and the trees, the men here were the natural inhabitants of the forests. But the education imparted by the Sahibs told those in power differently, and now they were hell-bent on the removal of the villagers.

Another important revelation was that the contract for providing the barbed wire fencing of the proposed sanctuary had been bagged by a multinational company called Vedang. That such a huge company had taken up such a paltry contract seemed rather strange. For years, there had been talk of building a processing plant for bauxite in this location, instead of it being carted outside. It seemed Vedang was coming in to have a sniff at the area. Vedang was a top deity of the Global Village. It was the story of the camel and the Arab all over again. The company was actually a foreign one but it had taken up a very Indian name, 'Vedang', showing how shrewd it was!

'The rascal Baba is interested in this issue because the local MP, who is also the state minister for forests at the centre, did not let him come close to him. Babaji had asked for funds from the MP quota to start a school, but MP Sahib overlooked his request. This had happened several times. Naturally, the rascal Baba is livid.' Their affiliation with two different political parties had added to the tension. Vidhayakji had planned to contest the MP election this time. As a matter of fact, both the rascal Baba and Vidhayakji were extremely sly. 'They must have got a sniff from the signboard of the company, Vedang, and realized that there would be big money involved. That was why they were eager to join the protest.

'We don't have to become a part of their muddle. We have to start our own battle and, this time, take care to avoid arrest. The police station would definitely declare us Naxalites.' Vedang had bribed them well.

The elders, baiga-pahans and pujar-mahtos from all the affected villages, gathered together for the meeting at Ambatoli. A new slogan was added to the standing demands: 'We shall die but not hand over our lands.'

The work at the mines stopped and the transport of bauxite ceased. Naturally, apprehension gripped the gods of the Global Village. It was doubly strong this time.

21

The Patharpaat outpost was teeming with policemen. Armed forces were stationed everywhere in the locality, but Lalchan Da, Doctor Ram Kumar and their colleagues were proving hard to trace. The administration was on the horns of a dilemma thanks to the pressure exerted by Vidhayakji and Shivdas Baba.

Lalchan Da's Samgharsh Samiti imposed a janta curfew on the paat. It was impossible for the police to venture into the villages. The police entered houses on the pretext of making arrests and molested the daughters and daughters-in-law. Sakhua trees were chopped down to build checkposts at the entry point to every village. A barrier made from a thick log lay across and blocked the width of the road. Stone weights were tied to one end, and the other end was pulled down with the help of strong ropes and tied to small stakes. There was no question of a vehicle passing through; there was only room enough to let in men, cattle or a bicycle on the flank. The checkposts were built in front of the houses of the Samgharsh Samiti members. If a police jeep ever came at night, the policemen had to stop and lift the barrier. Loud drums would start beating in the house and all the men and women of the village would gather within ten minutes. They would sit silently before the jeep. Sometimes, a havaldar or a sub-inspector would swear at them with mother and sister abuses, or prod them with his stick to incite them, but the silent and peaceful demonstration always compelled the police to go back.

The battle was being fought on Lalchan Da's strength, but he was now a ghost of his old self. He had changed; the murderer of his uncle had not been arrested yet, his finances had suffered terribly due to Balchan's treatment, and added to it was the humiliation his daughters had faced in the school. His laughter had vanished, and the glaze on his forehead had dulled. He paid little attention to the cleanliness of his clothes. The pride he had taken in belonging to the most prominent family on the paat, of being a man of influence, had taken a beating.

Since I was Lalita's sahiya now, my visits to Ambatoli had become more frequent, but Bhauji did not sing the dewar–bhabhi songs any longer. My sahiya would often hum the Phuljhar spring song, but could phool ever replace Bhauji?

Lalchan Da may also have been feeling alone because of Rumjhum's growing alcoholism. Doctor Sahib was preoccupied with his work. Wherever he went, the sick and the ailing from the paat hunted him down. He had to take care of his mother and sisters too. Soma or Bhikha could in no way replace Rumjhum for Lalchan Da. The only person who could fill the gap he left was my phool. But Kaka and the niece had never opened their hearts to one another. Since her childhood, Lalita had never talked freely with him. Everything was conveyed to him by Kaki. How could she dare to confront him directly? She had not grown that old yet, so she sat at the back during the meetings. Budhani Di tried many times to make her come to the front row, but she never agreed.

One day, Rumjhum and Lalita came to my room before I left for school. It turned out that, a year ago, Rumjhum had become a complete alcoholic. I heard that he used to rinse his mouth in the morning with the first produce of the mahua. His Baba did not live in Kandapaat anymore. He stayed at the school where he was posted, thirty kilometres from home. Sunil never came home from the university hostel. Ayo could not scold him; she could only mope, finding her son growing distant and emaciated. When Baba visited them on Sundays, Rumjhum kept away.

Today he was not drunk, probably because Lalita was visiting him. He sat silently for a while and spoke only after finishing the black lemon tea she had made. He said he needed the fax number for the Prime Minister's office. He had called Lalita early that morning to have a letter written to the Prime Minister. My eyes filled with tears when I went through it and a gasp rose in my breast. It had to be sent to the PMO. But getting hold of the fax number was not an easy job.

The strike had been on for more than a week. The senior officers began to visit the paat more frequently. The vehicles of Pandeyji and those of officials from Vedang kept roaring to and fro. Who could give me the fax number? I was at my wit's end. Rumjhum suggested I get it from MP Sahib. He had five odd pages full of official phone and fax numbers.

Right! Perfectly right. Who said he has gone off his rocker! There were more facts in his letter than ever came within the ken of newspaper readers like me.

The handwriting in the letter was beautiful, full of rounded letters—like pearls. I did not know the handwriting of my sahiya was as charming as she herself was. But the matter in the letter was extremely depressing, full of horrifying realities.

Respected Prime Minister,

Johar.

I had to fortify myself to write this letter to you. I have always been an admirer of your honesty and simplicity and have always thought very highly of you. I have been listening to the speeches you deliver on Independence Day and other occasions, broadcast by Akashvani.

There have been several times when you have candidly accepted the fact that people outside the market system have not been able to reap the benefits of this economy. You have been talking of lending a human face to the system. It has shone a ray of hope in our hearts.

Sir, you might know that our Asur community has been searching for the human face of governance for thousands of years.

When our ancestors took a vow to save the forests, they were called demons. When they resisted the burning of forests undertaken to expand agricultural fields, they were dubbed wicked fiends. They were attacked and chased away repeatedly.

But the defeat of the Asur community in the twentieth century has been our biggest rout in history. This time, not the Sing-Bonga of our legends, but companies like TATA have ruined us. Steel, hoes, trowels, digging bars and pick-axes made in their factories reach markets far away. Now nobody pays attention to the tools made from the steel smelted by us. Our age-old expertise of smelting steel has gradually disappeared.

In desperation, we took to agriculture and ploughed the bosom of the paat deity. However, legitimate and illegitimate bauxite mines are swallowing our land like a giant python.

Our daughters and our land are being taken away from us.

Where should we go now? It is beyond us to divine this.

In the capital, I once went to a slum near the university. I saw human beings, but they carried no faces. They were nameless. Their identities had been lost. I was beside myself with fear to see faceless human beings, sir. I ran off in horror.

Sir, maybe you know that there are hardly eight to nine thousand Asurs left alive now. We are scared. We don't want to become extinct. The wolf sanctuary will save the rare wolves, sir, but it will wipe out our race.

Truly speaking, we don't want to be faceless beings, sir. Rescue us, sir. You are our last ray of hope.

What more can I write?

Yours truly,
Rumjhum Asur
Kandapaat, PO Kanari
PS Koelbigha
Dist: Barwe, Kikat Pradesh.

My heart grew heavier as I read the letter again and again. Tears welled up in my eyes. I vowed silently to help this letter reach the PMO, come hell or high water.

22

Sakhuapaat was the largest weekly market in the area, but the closure of work in the mines had affected the traders badly. Still, shopkeepers came as usual and there was no shortage of customers. In the life of the tribals, the haat was not merely a marketplace but also a spot for social interaction. One could meet relatives from villages 10 to 15 kilometres away. When daughters-in-law met members from their naihar, or father's village, anyone could conclude from their delight that the meeting had taken place after a long gap. Marriages were fixed here and complaints were assuaged. News and gossip, of the life and death of kith and kin, were exchanged at the haat.

In the western corner of the haat, hanriya and wine were sold in a separate row. The boys' interest in cock fights had diminished now, but the charms of hanriya and wine persisted. There were dozens of people, like Rumjhum, who came here only to drink. The months of pent-up frustration would tumble out as soon as the wine made them tipsy. Naturally, fights were common.

The strategy for the battle was drawn up in a hut near the haat. The door to the hut stayed closed and men would work on the plans inside. The hut was quite crowded that day. Suddenly, the door crashed open and Soma stumbled in. One look at him confirmed that he had been bashed up mercilessly. Legs, arms, the back, ribs—every part of his body bore marks of the beating.

Doctor Sahib was galvanized into action. Dettol, ointments, dressings, injections—the treatment began on the spot. But Soma did not regain consciousness even half an hour after the injection had been administered. Doctor Sahib thoughtfully administered a bottle of glucose. Slowly, when he came to, he told them what had happened.

Soma had not been feeling well, so he had not come out for shopping on that day, staying back home in Ambatoli. Since it was a haat day, the village was empty, save for the elderly and the children. A police jeep arrived from the Patharpaat station and jawans dismounted to tear down the checkpost erected for the purpose of janta curfew. They had almost finished the demolition when Soma heard the noise from his room. He ran out to stop them, but they started hitting at him with canes, rifle butts and boots. When Baba ran up to pull Soma away, he was shoved so roughly that he hit a wall and fainted. Ayo came out and started crying. The old women from the neighbouring houses also began to raise a hue and cry. Only then did the policemen give up.

Dusk had fallen. There was no use going to the Patharpaat police station in the darkness. Perhaps the attack had even been a planned one. Darkness was a pretty convenient cover for the police. Everyone agreed to gherao the police station early the next morning. It was also decided that they would inform Vidhayakji so that the district magistrate and the SP could come down to listen to their grievances.

By eight the next morning, a huge crowd had collected round the Patharpaat police station. You could see nothing but men as far as the eyes travelled. Everyone sat down in their spots without any show of haste. There was no tension or hurry. All the men and the siyani folks of the paat had come prepared for the day-long picketing and gherao. They had only one demand they wanted to press: the policemen responsible for the unprovoked violence against Soma had to be suspended.

Vidhayakji arrived by ten. He walked into the police post and emerged half an hour later. He spoke with Lalchan Da and the others. The telephone at the post was out of order. He was unable to contact SP Sahib. He assured them that he had informed the officers before coming here. He walked off to his jeep, which was parked at a distance.

The policemen's ploy seemed to have been foiled. They had thought that the leaders of the Samgharsh Samiti would lose control after seeing Soma's condition and come to the police post that very night. But that did not happen. Now it was broad daylight, and here was this gigantic crowd. They were at their wit's end, unable to fathom how to tackle the mass who just sat there, peacefully.

I had the duty of keeping an eye on the situation from a tea stall nearby. The day seemed to be passing peacefully. But tension was building up inside the police post. Arrangements had been made for water and gram for the picketers. They looked quite relaxed. Right in front of the police post, powerfully built Balchan stood self-assuredly with Bhikha, Rumjhum and three of his friends. Even the police constables avoided meeting the eyes of this robust youth.

However, it was merely the lull before the storm. Needlessly, or perhaps deliberately, a burly police constable started talking nonsense at the paan shop. A couple of youths from the throng were there too. His tripe began to get unbearable for them.

'What do these Kol-curs, Asur-monkeys eat to become leaders? Do they even know what the word "leadership" means?'

'Arrey! If this was happening in my area, I would take out their heat in two minutes. Only last evening I trounced a boy in Ambatoli. He must have realized he has met somebody!'

'And look at these strumpets in heat of youth! Are they coming here to do dharna or to display their booby-goodies?'

'As if I don't know about these whores. There is not a single one among them whom I have not fucked.'

It was enough to test the patience of the boys. They slammed the constable down on the ground and began punching him. But the strong fellow broke away and ran to the police post, yelling loudly. By the time people could understand what was happening, he had taken out his rifle and started shooting at the crowd. And then the other constables opened fire.

I saw it all clearly from my spot. I saw Balchan lunge to snatch the rifle, but he tumbled down like a crashing tree. The men sitting in the front, including Rumjhum and Bhima, were shot dead. In the blink of an eye, there were six corpses lying there. A stampede broke out. The slope of the paat and the jungle lay beyond the open space opposite the post, and everyone ran towards it, helter-skelter.

The sight of the six dead bodies staggered even the police jawans. They stopped shooting. Only the constable who had been thrashed was still in a frenzy. He kept swearing and firing intermittently until the Officer-in-Charge came out to take him to task.

Budhani Di held Lalita and Doctor Sahib. Ram Kumar restrained Lalchan and pushed them to the cover of the trees, away from the bodies.

Whatever fell in the path of the retreating, frenzied mob was put to flames. The dumpers, trucks and offices of several mining companies were set ablaze. Lalita and

Budhani Di came across the clerk, Verma, and the peon, Dubey, from the Poddar mines. The two were pounded severely. The leaders of the Samgharsh Samiti melted into the jungle. In policespeak, they went 'underground'.

Meanwhile, while the Officer-in-Charge and the old havaldar of the police outpost were considering ways to dispose of the dead bodies, they realized to their horror that these were not flesh and bone and were rapidly disappearing. When they crept closer, they saw only molten steel, seeping slowly into the soil. They were so scared that they abandoned the post and ran away.

The next morning, the newspapers did not report the news of the butchery. The story of a handsome cricketer hitting six sixes in a single over drowned out everything else. Then there was the usual fare—statements and assurances given by leaders, press releases of bureaucrats and NGOs, programmes of different political parties, local civic problems, and so on. Of course, on page three, there was a story that ran into two columns, that of six Naxalites being shot dead in a police encounter at Patharpaat. The notorious area commander, Balchan, was said to be one of those killed. There were also details of the brutal crimes committed by him—a list of the murders of SPs and police inspectors and the bank robberies, a running commentary. In the last paragraph, however, it was mentioned that the retreating Naxalites had carried away the dead bodies of their comrades. The police force was still, allegedly, searching for the corpses.

23

My cheek resting in my palm, I reclined on the chowki. Gandoor sat in the chair opposite me; Etwari and her nervous children were seated below on the mat. I had two papers in my hands. One was Rumjhum's letter to the Prime Minister, the other was a show cause notice from the district education officer, asking for an explanation for my connivance with criminals.

The unremitting series of incidents had broken us. The leaders of the Samgharsh Samiti had left the area. All the older boys and girls had also quit the paat and left to escape arrest and torture. Only the children and the old folks were left in the village. They had to bear the brunt of the police brutality. If one headed towards the west, a journey of barely four or five hours on foot would be enough to take one to another state. The paat people had relatives on that side too.

In spite of the restlessness of the high-flying Global Gods, there seemed to be no immediate solution for the mining companies. There were many miners among those who had run away out of terror. Naturally, work could not start in the mines. The companies had suffered a lot of damage at the hands of the retreating mob. Vedang was also facing problems, now that workers were in short supply. However, the wheeler-dealers were still active, trying to push things forward.

Shivdas Baba and Vidhayakji had guessed correctly that a substantial company like Vedang would not have jumped into the fray simply to erect a barbed wire fence. In fact, it turned out that the company needed hundreds of acres to set up its plant in the coal region. MP Sahib had set things right for himself in the capital. It was he who had proposed the three-point agenda in the garb of petty contract work. Now Babaji and Vidhayakji's shares had to be finalized.

The two knew that land was as inalienable a part of industry as capital, technology and labour. Since land could not be made available in Koelbigha without their help, they expected to receive their share in the company. On the other hand, the company had not in its wildest dreams considered offering them a share. Thanks to their squabbling, the fight on the paat grew fiercer. The rascal Baba and the MLA then seized another opportunity to strike a bargain. They promised support in crushing the crusade if the company agreed to give them shares. The terms were agreed upon in a cosy air-conditioned room in a five-star hotel in Mumbai. The two agreed to an astronomical sum they had never imagined in the past or dreamt of in the future. They had shot an arrow in the dark, and it was sheer chance that it hit the sweet spot. Babaji believed in the adage that a woman's character and a man's destiny cannot be divined even by the gods, let alone petty mortals.

Bells of jubilation began to peal. The gods blew their conches in victory. The police dismantled the janta curfew barrier at Ambatoli and beat Soma up. A chain reaction of incidents and accidents were then set into motion.

Sunil came back to Kandapaat. The dates of the examination had not been announced yet. The news of Rumjhum's murder had agitated him terribly. But his Baba found his presence in the village worrying. He had also been lingering in the village, neglecting his duties at school. The pain of a young son's death weighed on his chest. He had gone mute, and his eyes were always moist. He was neither bothered about his clothes nor the passage of time. He wanted Sunil to go back to his hostel as quickly as possible. He didn't think he should be present in the village or the paat. His left eye twitched ominously. He was not ready to lose another son. But Sunil was unwilling to leave him alone in such a precarious situation. Finally, in protest, Baba stopped eating food or drinking water. Sunil had no choice but to return to the hostel.

The pressure on me also grew by the day. Letters arrived from home, one after the other. Babuji and my uncle nearly staged a picket at the MLA's house. The news of the Naxal business and firing had reached them. Ma and Babuji were not as terrified of ghosts and ghouls as they were of Naxalites. Babuji wanted me transferred to another place at any cost. People who visited my house to seek my hand in marriage backed out the moment Barwe district and Koelbigha were mentioned. No visitor would come to my home if Sakhuapaat or Bhaunrapaat were brought up. Babuji was convinced the only alternative was to have me moved quickly.

Rumjhum's letter was lying on my table, and his echoing, melancholic song prevented me from even dreaming of another option. Many times, I had resolved to take this fight to its logical conclusion. From each atom of the paat, from each bough and leaf of sakhua, from the blood-red palaash, I could hear Rumjhum's lament resonating:

Our night
Assures us
It will be a sinister, gloomy night
…………..
………….
Sad winds
Lament somewhere far off
………….
………….

On our heels
Treads our Nemesis
A wounded deer
Hearing the running steps of his hunter pursuing him
Readies itself
For Absolute Death.

Can Death too be charming? Does Destiny usher in defeat too? I brooded. Then why was it that, not only in this Kikat Pradesh, but in other states as well, communities on the margin were struggling to survive? Were they heading towards Absolute Death? Didn't the newspapers, magazines and journals carry such reports day in and day out?

Following privatization, a large river called Shivnath, flowing through the Durg district of Chhattisgarh, had been sold off to an industrial group. Natives from a number of villages, the cattle, birds, farms and fields were parched. The inhabitants of Bonda Tikragaon staged a sit-down protest in the capital. Two women, Satyabhama and Shaura, also joined the fast with their husbands and children. The powers that be thought the matter was not worth paying attention to, because the picketing was not being staged by a rich or powerful person. Moreover, for people who survived on a single meal a day, of what significance was their hunger strike? It was no wonder that Satyabhama and Shaura died from hunger on the eve of

Independence Day. Those in power thought it was a fine poverty-control measure, so following this, another three or four rivers were put into private hands.

Thirty-four-year-old Irom Sharmila, daughter of Irom Nanda and Irom Sakhi, has been on a fast unto death for the last seven years in protest against the Special Rights Act favouring the armed forces. She was barely 15 kilometres from Imphal, the capital of Manipur. The act gave the forces the authority to open fire without warning at any gathering of five or more people, and ironically, those attacked could not ask for judicial redress. Irom Sharmila has been in police custody ever since. She is being force-fed fluids though her nose. Reduced to a skeleton, her body is refusing even fluids now. Absolute Death stares her in the face.

C.K. Janu of Kerala, the leader of 53,000 tribal families uprooted due to the obduracy of the Forest Department, suffered police brutality when she and her followers tried to settle on the gair-majurwa land in Vaind district.

Surekha Dalvi, the leader of 13,000 displaced tribal families in the Konkan region of Maharashtra; Duvasia Devi battling it out in the Rewa district of Madhya Pradesh; Daya Bai working in a Gond village in Chhindwara, Madhya Pradesh—how many stories do we have to tell, and for how long?

Earth is a woman, Nature is a woman, Sarna Mai is a woman; fighting for them, Satyabhama, Irom Sharmila,

C.K. Janu, Surekha Dalvi and Budhani Di here on the paat, as well as my sahiya, Lalita, are all women. Maybe only a woman can understand another woman. Daughters are like Sita—always prepared to unite with the earth. This makes the hunter, the man, superfluous.

24

On Saturday, Gandoor and I walked till it was nearly midnight. It is hard to say how many valleys we descended and how many paats we crossed to finally reach Lalita's mausi's house, where the family was hiding. The village was in the middle of a forest, beyond the borders of Kikat Pradesh. Lalita expressed neither happiness nor sadness at my arrival. Calamities and unrelenting tension had soaked away the elixir of our lives. She had been no less attached to Balchan than to Lalchan Ka. She had spent her childhood perched on his shoulders during visits to the haat-bazaar, the fields and the farms, the hills and the jungles. She felt like an orphan now. She had to be worried about her future too, as she had selected a dreadful adversary for herself. The ruler had given them a taste of his power. Perhaps she was also afraid of her own weakness.

She had had nothing to do but mull over what had happened since coming here. After all, how long does it take to cook for two people, her Mausa and Mausi? Her study of history had taught her that there was no effective counter measure to nation-state violence. She believed that the bricks of violence had built not only the foundation of the state, but that its palaces had also been built from the same material. The state was the only establishment that had institutionalized bloodshed. Its armed forces, paramilitary forces, the police—every organ of the state was steeped in the doctrine of destruction. The nation-state used humans to kill their fellows in order to protect itself. Budgets running into millions and billions were officially allocated for the purpose. Research projects were undertaken to find ways and means to slaughter the largest numbers in the shortest time. In this world, there are few species that prey on their own kind. The nation-state had turned man into a cannibal who felt no guilt. It was its unique feature.

Lalita was sorry for the ransacking that had been done by the irate villagers. It was not right. It had weakened their position in the fight and they had been forced to pull back. The lords of the Global Village had been waiting impatiently for an opportunity like that to display their real might. And we had handed them the chance on a platter, like total idiots.

We both agreed that the high-flying global deities and the nation-state had merged together, and it was now difficult to tell them apart. It was common knowledge now who held the strings of the puppets dancing on stage.

Normally, when the high-flying gods watch the

minerals, jungles and other resources of Chhattisgarh, Odisha, Madhya Pradesh or Jharkhand from their sky routes, or through the lenses of satellites, they are confident that this is their personal property. They know well that they are the nation-state and therefore, its resources belong only to them. Naturally, when they see the loincloth-clothed Asur-Birijia, Oraon and Munda tribals, Dalits and Sadaans around the mineral resources and the jungles, they get irritated, and grow impatient to exterminate the insects—to begin Operation Mop-up.

The wounded deer are waiting for Absolute Death.

The chilling realization depressed me. Meanwhile, Gandoor smoked away a whole bundle of biris, but at least he was listening attentively. He did not budge from his spot. Lalchan Da and Doctor Sahib were not there. Somebody told me Ramchan was suffering from diarrhoea. The constantly changing water and food in different places had, perhaps, not agreed with him. He was in a bad shape and had to be carried on a string cot. It took around two hours to reach the market outside the jungle. There was a clinic there, and a couple of medical shops. Since it was Chhattisgarh, there was nothing to fear.

We had dinner and fell asleep while arguing over the ways and means to unite our scattered cadre.

25

Lalchan Da and Doctor Ram Kumar had just stepped onto the road, along with the two boys who carried Ramchan on the cot. They had hardly walked half a mile when four police jeeps surrounded them. The Barwe district police and the Chhattisgarh police had undertaken a joint operation and the informer who had tipped them off that day had been their most reliable one. His information had never been proven wrong.

The police picked up Ram Kumar and Lalchan, leaving Ramchan in the care of the two boys. They were seated in separate vehicles. The jeeps moved in opposite directions and entered the forest. Lalchan and Doctor Sahib were not only told that they would be killed in fake encounters, but they also heard the sound of the guns being fired. It was the strategy the police used to break their morale. Their faces turned ashen. They felt extremely alone, and were on the verge of breaking.

Lalchan Da was seen for only a day in the Koelbigha lock-up, after which he vanished without a trace.

Lalita and I got the news the very next day. It was hard to believe the report of the encounter. The two boys had somehow taken Ramchan to the doctor's. They managed the expenses for the intravenous administration of glucose and brought him back the following day.

The work in the mines was still halted because there was a huge shortage of labourers. Vedang had also been unable to start its fencing project. The restlessness of the gods mounted. Bringing labourers from outside and maintaining them on the paat would have meant four times their proposed expenditure. They were not willing to bear such huge expenses. As long as there was bauxite on the paat, they needed people in the villages for cheap labour, but they did not want any trouble.

The month of Asharh brought a ray of hope to the gods. Now the villagers were bound to return. Cultivation could not be left to the children and the aged. A project for the rain season potato was introduced on the paat.

The junior officer at the Koelbigha Block, the BDO and his staff, broke into a frenzy all of a sudden. The agriculture officer, the jan sewak—everyone trooped to the paat. Why? Because the rain season potato had to be cultivated. All the families on the paat had to do it, whether they were Asurs, Birijia or Korba—the seeds had been bought at full subsidy. Tongues wagged, saying that the government had borne the total cost of the seeds, eleven lakh rupees, and that of the fertilizers, seven lakhs. A tribal family could take as many seeds as it wanted.

The block officers, who never had deigned to take a peep at the paat, now camped there for two or three days in a row. The community hall at Ambatoli was bustling. Truckloads of potato seeds were carted into the hall.

As expected, the inhabitants of the paat began to return. Lalita, Budhani Di, Ramchan—everyone came back. Lalita was surprised to see that the block office, which had never ventured beyond distributing blankets, mosquito nets, he-goats and she-goats, had come up with the idea of potato cultivation. How had they begun to see us as farmers, she asked, when they had always viewed us as beggars before? Or, at the most, as people begging for the bounty of the Indira Awaas Yojana's welfare schemes.

The officers would laugh in derision if you spoke of tanks or wells. 'Tanks and ponds on top of the mountain! Are you crazy?' You could try your best to convince them that sizeable ponds could be dug in the larger basins between the two paats, where the Asurs had their paddy fields, but nobody would listen. If they had come this far, they should have visited the interior regions; then they might have gotten an idea. The junior staff did visit, but why would their superiors listen to their reports?

The senior bureaucrats in the capital owned large plantations of pears in Patharpaat, some as large as twenty acres. When the trees filled with pears, they were auctioned off. Fruit traders from as far as the capital came down for the auction. They could make a profit of lakhs in a single stroke! But there were never any plans to develop pear plantations in Asur villages. Who would bear the expenses? Suppose bauxite deposits were found in those very spots? Who wanted to face the brunt of the accounts audit?

Take up cultivation this year with the seeds supplied by the government, the villagers were told. The cooperative will purchase the potato and put the money in the bank in your name. The following year, potato cultivation would have to be done with this capital. Money could not be withdrawn from the account till then, even if the villagers were dying of hunger.

How would the Asurs take up cultivation the next year with the money received from the sale of the potato harvest this year? The bureaucrats did not have an answer. Would waving incense sticks before the money deposited in the bank meet the expenses incurred in times of illness and disease, the visits of guests and hospitality, fees and medicine, rice and vegetables? No, it would have to be taken out of the bank. Only folks with full bellies could make such ill-thought-out plans. The whole thing was not at all practical. The officers realized it but they had orders from above, so they protested their helplessness.

Anyway, the paat hummed with life again. It was not like the early times, but men could be seen now. The operations in the mines began once more. The deities believed things would return to normal. It is natural to forget one's past anxieties. Time is an excellent healer.

But the houses of men like Lalchan Da, Rumjhum and Ram Kumar stood desolate. Only the wind moved around here. Their Ayos kept asking the visitors to the town and the markets about their sons. Rumjhum's Ayo did not have any idea of his seeping into the soil, even now. Doctor Sahib's mother found it difficult to protect her grown-up daughters from the evil eye of thugs like Ansari.

Moving from this location to that, from that to this, blindfolded in the moving police jeep night after night, bearing torture and beatings, Lalchan was shattered. Misleading him was a part of the strategy. The news of the deaths of Ram Kumar, Ramchan, Lalita and Budhani Di, one after the other, the non-stop whipping, the thirst and hunger, all of it took away his reasoning. He was unable to remember how many months this had been going on. Often, he would forget his own name. When the perpetrators were convinced this half-crazy, half-dead Lalchan was of no more use to them, his signature was forcibly taken on a blank piece of paper and he was finally released.

By the time he made his way back home, a new tractor had been dispatched to his house in Ambatoli. The Shindalco manager, Pandeyji, announced breezily that Lalchan Asur had come to an agreement with the company and had disbanded the Samgharsh Samiti. Now there would be no closure-*shlosure*. Vedang would commence its fencing work.

Lalchan being given a new tractor, a petty contractorship in the mine and a plot to build a house in the town? At first nobody believed it. But those who had seen the gleaming new tractor at his gates were taken in.

The story spread like wildfire in the Sakhuapaat haat. All the villagers wilted. It was like a blow from the news of one's own death.

'How can it be?'

'James and Lalchan weren't alike.'

'Did Lalchan Da learn treachery in the company of that rascal Shivdas Baba?'

The questions tormented everyone but there was no answer to any of them.

Lalchan Da managed to reach Sakhuapaat, but things had already changed. Men avoided his eyes. There were no greetings, no johar. They refused to acknowledge him. He felt he had come to the wrong place. His face and physique had become so gaunt that it was hard to recognize him. But the hatred was in their eyes, thanks to the report of his treachery, although he had no inkling of it.

He felt something was amiss when he saw the new tractor at the gates. But by the time he could ask, Balchan's wife stumbled out and fell on the tractor. She started banging her head on it, all the while wailing loudly, as though it were not a tractor but Balchan's dead body. Baba came out of his room and spat on the tractor. Lalchan felt like he had been spat on.

Nobody enquired after his welfare. Nobody tried to find out how he had borne the months in police custody. Nobody offered to wash his feet. On the contrary, they walked out of the house, one by one. Even his own gomkain, Namita and Kavita's mother. The children left too.

Lalchan Da felt it would have been better if he had been shot dead by the police. What kind of blow was this, that his own kith and kin had turned strangers? In no time at all, not only his own family, but the relatives living in the neighbourhood had also vacated their houses. They not only vacated the houses, but also ripped off the thatched roofs and demolished the ovens. He had been ostracized. Now he was alone. He had become an untouchable for his community and society.

He hit himself on the breast and toppled down on the earth. His chest heaved with soundless sobs. He shed enough tears to wet the soil around him.

When darkness fell, I walked silently to Lalchan Da. He had fallen asleep, weeping, on the ground outside his door. He started when I woke him. I took him in my arms and began to stroke him and maybe he recognized me from my touch. He had gone mute. I had brought him khichadi in a tiffin box. At my insistence, he ate a couple of morsels, and then broke into tearful cries. I, too, began to sob. His golden physique had been reduced to an ashen skeleton. What tortures the man had suffered!

He was suffering even now, after coming home. Was he receiving his punishment for sins committed in a previous birth? The more I thought, the faster the tears rolled down my cheeks.

26

I sat by Lalchan Da, trying to comfort him, caressing his palms between my own. He finally fell asleep late that night. I went home. Nightmares tormented me, disturbing my sleep. I got up repeatedly to sip water. Threatening, black storms, cruel clouds and tempests raged in my dreams. I saw a fire consuming everything around me. They were leaping flames, hungry to turn everything into ashes, and I staggered amidst the flares. Was I trying to find someone in the middle of the crackling, raging fire? Molten steel flowed by—red, burning steel. It was the steel that had surged after the Patharpaat shooting. Rumjhum, Balchan, Doctor Ram Kumar—everyone entered my dream one by one, shouting loudly, trying to explain something to me. But I neither heard their words in the blast nor followed their gestures. Apart from images of dread and fear, I saw nothing.

I got up late the next morning, feeling jaded. My left eye twitched persistently. I felt drained, as though someone had wrung my mind and body like a wet piece of cloth.

I lay in bed, mulling over the dream. Suddenly, I started missing everyone terribly—Doctor Ram Kumar, Balchan, Rumjhum, everyone. They were needed here so badly. Lalchan or Rumjhum would have taken care of everything. Lalchan Da would not have had to endure his fate alone. Ram Kumar could have convinced everybody on the paat, the entire community.

Be it Vedang or any other industrial group, none would have dared to bring outsiders to resume the fencing work if Balchan or Rumjhum were here. I remembered Rumjhum's statements. He always emphasized that the weak could not survive in this world. They would be systematically annihilated, like the Native Americans. Whatever the Spanish, Dutch, French and the British had done to the Native Americans earlier had happened to this community too, and it was happening again. The terrible silence of history could not deny it.

Rumjhum had once told me that no other example in world history could match the barbaric manner in which the Spanish had destroyed the Incan and the Aztec civilizations. The Spanish could not tolerate a culture that was more advanced than their own. The sight of them made the Spanish all the more brutal. The Aztecs' knowledge of mathematics, their astronomy-based calendar, town planning, traffic system, census, civil registration methods and education were far ahead of those of the Spanish. As a result, they were wiped out in cold blood.

The Native Americans had also considered all Europeans intruders. But what could we say about the present times? The global deities of today are above the concerns of ethnicity, race, colour and gender. Such paltry issues do not impress them. Their vision is clear. They want abundant ore, most of the land, profuse forests, the resources of water and electricity, plenty of factories, a plethora of products and full profits. They do not discriminate between their own and strangers, the native and the alien, in their effort to achieve these objectives.

The reality was that Balchan and Rumjhum were gone forever. Where was Ram Kumar? Was he alive or dead? Was there any assurance that if someone were to make enquiries at the police station, he would not be thrown behind bars? I remembered Sunil. He would have proven a great help. Lalita and Budhani Di would have received strong support. The absence of Ram Kumar and Rumjhum would have been mitigated, a little. But his Baba—who could defy his obstinate command?—would never let him stay on the paat. Lalchan Da was there, but he was useless.

Perhaps I could take an initiative. I could tell Lalita and Budhani Di the heartrending story that was conveyed in Lalchan Da's tears. The true story behind the tractor, and the bragging lies of the manager, Pandeyji. I should hold nothing back.

But would anyone listen? Everyone burst into a rage as soon as Lalchan Da's name was uttered. Lalita and Budhani

Di glared as if they could burn you alive with their stares. When I timidly tried to tell Lalita and Budhani Di the next day, they refused to listen to me. They were more concerned with the fencing being done by the labourers from Vedang. They felt it was a sin to hear the name of Lalchan Da.

I thought I would mention it a few days later. I would speak when things improved, I told myself. The Asurs of the forest villages, Kherwar–Sadaan—everyone was on the edge. The hut by Budhani Di's desi cabin and the haat had begun to fill up again. Lalita and Budhani Di were in the lead.

They resolved, after a lengthy discussion, that the fencing would not be allowed to take place without compensation, rehabilitation and other necessary arrangements. Why should they bother what the khaitan says? The government could clearly see that thousands of families inhabited these villages. Where would they go? The negotiations had to begin.

They also decided that there would be no crowd or procession—only fifteen to twenty people would go for the talks. Everything would be put down in the application. There would not be too many arguments. No conflicts. They would press only for compensation and rehabilitation.

Vedang Company, the police and the administration were informed that the negotiators would arrive the following day to meet the authorities; work must not resume till then.

They had the appointment at the Vedang Company office, two miles away from Sakhuapaat, at ten the next morning. Around nine, Lalita called out from the outer gate of the school: 'Hey, phooool! Come, it's almost time!'

I had heard the sweet call after a gap of months—and it was honey pouring into my ears! But Etwari ran up and shackled my door from the outside. I kept begging and pleading with her to open the door. But she stood against it, adamant, sobbing loudly. A bristling Gandoor hurried away. Etwari brought a sturdy log and jammed it against the door. By then, Gandoor had clambered onto Etwa's truck. Lalita, Budhani Di and the others were already there. Etwari also made a dash for it and scrambled up before the truck could leave.

About ten minutes after they left, the little girls from the hostel undid the chain and removed the log on the door. I stepped out. Pedalling frantically on my bicycle, I had not even reached Sakhuapaat when I heard the sound of loud explosions. Startled, I fell off. I felt I would never be able to get back on my feet again. My chest heaved with suppressed sobs. I had a premonition that I would never see any of them alive—Lalita, Etwari, Budhani Di, no one. But the noise was not the clatter of bullets. Were they using bombs and grenades? How can one throw bombs at unarmed people? Which police, which military has turned so brutal? Paranoia shrieked in my ears, telling me that the vicious killers had butchered them all. The soft call of 'Hey, phooool' was lost forever. Everyone was dead, but for me! Why had Etwari kept me from joining them? Why did not she care for her innocent babies? Why did she try to protect me? Why didn't she stop Gandoor? The children, the paat, the Asurs, the tribal community—they were all orphans. And I? But there was no one to answer my cries. A river of tears poured down my face, set to the deafening noise.

My misgivings, the gasps, the pounding heartbeats and tears could not stop me. I blundered on. The explosions resounded, echoing against the surrounding hills. My ears were stunned. My legs were trembling. Somehow bracing myself, I started moving slowly.

Later, I was told that landmines had been laid on the road to the office. Fifteen bodies, including those of Lalita, Budhani Di, Gandoor, Etwari and Lalchan's Baba, had been blown to pieces. But instead of blood, molten steel had begun to flow from the bodies. Red, liquid steel seeped into the soil of the paat. After Patharpaat, it had happened once again. The hot steel flowed by my feet too, drawing me like a strong magnet.

The gods of the Global Village were delirious with joy. The battle that had commenced in the Vedic Age, the same battle that thousands of Indras had not been able to end, had now been won by the deities of the Global Village.

Asur-Birijia, Birhor-Korba, the tribal communities, all the aborigines would now be part of the mainstream, the waves of which were leaping up to lap up the moon. Winding through the capitals of various states, the swell rushed through Delhi to Washington DC.

Luxuriant woods of palaash swayed where the molten steel had flowed on the paat. Waves of heat radiated from the ruby-red palaash. Searing waves, as from molten, gushing steel!

Sunil Asur walked out of the university hostel in the capital, in the company of his friends. He would have to take over the reins of the war.

Glossary

Asuri = A
Bengali = B
Bhojpuri = Bh
Hindi = H
Magahi = M
Sanskrit = S
Urdu = U

Aaji (A)	grandmother
Abhayaranya (S)	sanctuary
Akhra (A)	a meeting hall
Alta (B)	a red cosmetic decoration on the palms and the soles of the feet
Amaltas (A)	laburnum, a tree with bunches of bright yellow flowers
Anganbadi (H)	literally, 'courtyard shelter'; the name of a programme begun by the Government of India to provide basic health amenities to rural women and children

Arkanthe (A)	adamantine
Asharh (H)	a month in the Hindu calendar corresponding to June/July of the Gregorian calendar
Asur (A, H)	a tribe in Jharkhand
Ayo (A)	mother
Baiga (A)	witch man
Barahil (Bh, M)	a kind of bonded labour, minion
Bhaat-jhor (A, B)	boiled rice and gravy
Bhabhi (H)	sister-in-law
Bhabho (A)	wife's brother
Bhagat (A)	priest
Bhang (H)	drink made from cannabis
Bhauji (A)	sister-in-law
Bir (A)	brother
Bundiya (H)	small, fried balls of gram flour, filled with sugary syrup
Chote Sahib (H)	Junior Master
Chowki (H)	a wooden bed
Chuan (A)	a spring
Chunar (H)	a cloth used as a veil or drape
Da (B)	an informal term for brother, short form of Dada

Dewar (H)	a term for younger brother-in-law
Dhenki (A)	a wooden stick used to pound paddy
Dhuska (Bh)	fried patties made from ground rice and lentil batter
Don (A)	a fertile area of cultivated land in a valley that receives plenty of water
Dona (H)	a leaf bowl
Gair majurwa (H)	literally 'without deed', ie: without legal papers to prove an individual's ownership, and so becomes owned by the government. Such lands generally include pastures, wasteland, roads and ponds, which have often been used or cultivated for generations and are hence owned de facto, or are well-utilized community lands
Gandoor (A)	garbage heap
Ghughuni (B)	a preparation of chickpeas
Ghunna (H)	nickname for a quiet person
Gomkain (A)	wife
Gotra (S)	clan
Gulainchi (A)	plumeria; a sweet-smelling flowering tree
Gulgula (Bh)	small, round, sweet wheat fritters
Gutka (H)	a mixture of chewing tobacco and ground areca nut

Haat (A)	a marketplace and meeting point
Halka karamchari (H)	a junior block-level officer
Hanriya (A)	country liquor
Hariyari (A)	harvest festival
Havaldar (H)	constable
Homa (S)	a fire ceremony
Jadura (A)	a tribal dance performed in the season between Karma and Sarhul festivals
Jamunia (A)	literally, jamun-coloured, amethyst, a woman's name
Jan curfew (H)	curfew imposed by the people, instead of by the authorities
Jan sewak (H)	a junior village-level officer
Janani (H)	one who bears children
Jhoomar (A)	a tribal dance
Jhum (A)	a shifting method of cultivation in which brush growth and trees are slashed and burnt to make agricultural fields
Johar (A)	tribal greeting
Ka (H)	an informal term for uncle, short for Kaka
Kachari (A, H)	a gram-flour fritter

Kaner (H)	Indian oleander, a tree with bright flowers
Karam (A)	a festival observed by the tribal and non-tribal communities of Jharkhand in which branches of the karam tree are propitiated
Katta (H)	country-made pistol
Khaini (H)	a form of chewing tobacco, mashed with lime
Khaitan (H)	a land document
Kharif (U)	one of the two crop-growing seasons in North India
Khasra (H, U)	identifying unit for a piece of land in land records
Khata (U)	identifying unit for a piece of land in land records
Khichadi (H)	a preparation of rice and pulses
Khira (H)	cucumber
Koynaar (A)	an edible herb
Langta (H)	naked
Lathait (H)	henchman with bamboo staff
Maandar (A)	a drum-like percussion instrument, hung from the neck of the performer
Mahto (A)	a headman

Mahua (H)	country liquor made from the mahuwa (*madhuca longifolia*) tree's blossoms
Maidan (H)	an open area, often used as a gathering place
Malgujari (U)	land tax
Mausa (H)	a term used for the mother's sister's husband
Mausi (H)	a term used for the mother's sister
Mouja (U)	identifying unit for a piece of land in land records
Munshi (H)	a head clerk
Muharrir (U)	a junior clerk
Murikatwa (A)	traditional head-hunter
Naihar (A)	father's village
Oal (B)	elephant's-foot yam
Paat (A)	plateau
Pahan (A)	high priest
Pajhara (A)	small waterfalls
Palaash (H)	*Butea monosperma*, flame of the forest tree, with bright red curved flowers
Panchayat sewak (H)	a village-level employee
Phool (H)	flower
Piyazi (H)	fritters made with shredded onions

Pujar (A)	priest
Rabi (U)	one of the two crop-growing seasons in North India
Raiyat/i (U)	a person who has acquired holding rights for land for cultivation; land owned by such a person
Raqba (U)	identifying unit for a piece of land in land records
Sadaans (H)	original non-tribal inhabitants of Jharkhand
Sadasi-Kutasi (A)	harvest festival
Sahiya (A)	partner, friend
Sakhua (A)	*Shorea robusta*, a species of tree with large leaves, often used for timber
Samdhi (H)	term for a daughter's or son's father-in-law, used by his or her parents
Sarguja (H)	a kind of grain
Sarhul (A)	tribal New Year festival
Sarna (A)	holy orchard
Seer (H)	a measurement of weight
Sev (H)	fried gram-flour vermicelli
Sindoor (H)	vermillion powder
Siyani (H)	a sagacious woman
Sohrai (A)	a tribal festival; also decorative art in which outer walls of the house are

	decorated with nature-oriented paintings
Sur (S)	non-Asur
Taand (A)	a less fertile area of cultivated land at the top of the hill that does not hold much water
Tahsildar (U)	land revenue officer
Thaan (A)	a site for the propitiation of a particular god or goddess
Thana (U)	police station
Tola (H)	generally a caste-based settlement, locality
Urad (H)	a kind of pulse
Yajna (S)	a fire sacrifice ceremony